Blood of a Red Rose

Book two of The Rose Trilogy

Blood of a Red Rose

by

Tish Thawer

Amber Leaf Publishing

Divide, Colorado

First Edition
First Printing, 2012
ISBN: 978-0-9856703-0-6

Library of Congress Control Number: 2012909481

Cover design by Regina Wamba of Mae I Design and Photography
Free stock photo of woman courtesy of Marcus Ranum /ranum.com
Edited by Kara Malinczak

Amber Leaf Publishing, Divide, Colorado
www.amberleafpublishing.com
www.tishthawer.com

ACKNOWLEDGEMENTS

To my wonderful family whose support means the world to me: I love you.

To Cortney, my friend and confidant: thank you for always listening to my ideas, shooting down the crappy ones, and shaking your pom-poms for the good ones.

To my amazing cover artist and friend, Regina Rasmussen Wamba: thank you for all you do, and for sharing my need for perfection.

To my fantastic editor Kara Malinczak: thanks for being tough! *wink*

PROLOGUE

Our New Life

(Rose)

By the time we reached The Rising Pit, my eyes were dry. I literally couldn't cry anymore. Just a few hours ago, everything had been so perfect. My dad had broken up with that demon bitch, I had finally gained back my freedom, and we were going to go buy me a new car the following day.

But in a flash, everything had changed. I found out my mom had been murdered by a demon who was after my father, because apparently he was a demon, too. And not only was I a demon as well, but now...I was also a murderer.

I hadn't thought twice about killing Meredith when Christian told me to do it. Not only had I wanted revenge for my mother, but also I had to keep her from telling Christian that I was a demon.

I had no idea how I knew it, but when Meredith had admitted to killing my mom, I felt the rage inside of me rise to the point where something physically changed within me. It was like I felt my DNA shifting. So when she told me that my father and I were demons, I knew she was telling the truth. I also knew she was telling the truth about Christian's clan wanting to kill me if they found out.

I wasn't sure how I was going to keep this secret, but then again, I had always been able to keep my thoughts hidden. *My God, that was it!* After learning about the effects of Meredith's blood on Terrance and how it kept his thoughts protected and *fuzzy*, it all made sense. No wonder I never had a problem hiding my thoughts from Evie...it was because of my demon blood.

"Rose? Are you going to be okay?" Christian's question startled me out of my inner turmoil. With everything racing around in my head, all I could do was nod in response.

"I know what happened is something that's going to take some time to process. But you have to realize, you didn't have a choice. She killed your mom and could have hurt you or your dad. She infected Terrance and there was no way I could let her threaten anyone else in my family. Killing her was the right thing to do."

He shifted in his seat and took both of my hands in his. "We need to get you inside and tell Evie everything that happened, but first I need to ask you a question. You know you can no longer go back to your old life, right? I'm sorry, but I won't let you be placed in a situation where you could be taken from me. I love you and I never want to live without you." He swallowed hard and cupped my cheek in his palm. "I will soon become the new Sire, and when I am I want you to be my consort. If you agree, I'm sure Evie will let you stay here with us from now on. We can start our new life together right away."

Oh my God. This was what I had been dreaming of for so long, but how was this going to work? I was a demon and Christian wanted me to become his consort. It was going to kill me to have to tell him I couldn't become a vampire anymore...that I could never be his consort.

I was so scared and I knew I would never be able to go home again. Staying with the clan seemed like the best way to stay protected. They could bite and use their sedative on anyone who came looking for me. It was the obvious choice, even if it wasn't for the same reasons as Christian thought. "Yes. I would love to stay with you and the clan. Thank you, Christian. You are truly saving my life."

"You are my life Rose, and I'll gladly spend an eternity proving that to you." He leaned over and kissed me. It was soft, tender, and filled with emotion.

The pain in my heart left me feeling like I was the one with a poker through my chest. How could I live with the man I loved while planning to lie to him every single day?

I guess I was about to learn *exactly* how to break a vampire's heart...

Rose's eyes close, and the darkness sets in,

How can I live with my lover as a friend?

* * * * *

CHAPTER ONE

Changed

(Rose)

Killing my dad's ex-girlfriend and living with Christian's vampire clan had been the best decision I'd ever made. I was able to spend my nights with the love of my life, and fill my days finishing my college courses online while they slept. I'd graduated on time and had now passed my twenty-first birthday. The only downfall...I really missed my dad.

"Rose, are you okay?" It wasn't Christian's question that startled me; it was, once again, the shock of how beautiful he was, and that I was a part of his everyday life now. My dreams had come true. He was my angel on earth.

My mouth started to water as my eyes scanned him from top to bottom. He was standing there with a towel wrapped around his waist. Fresh from the shower, his light blonde highlighted hair was wet, and his caramel eyes were sparkling with golden rays that could've been straight from the sun. He was so perfect, and damn did he have the most gorgeous body...one I'd become very familiar with over the past four months. All things considered, I was a very lucky girl.

I pushed myself off our bed and wrapped my arms around him. "I was just thinking about everything that's happened. Terrance, Meredith, my dad. I...I just can't believe how much everything has changed."

He pulled out of my hug, kissed me on the lips, and then looked deep into my eyes. "I know, baby, but now you're living and working here full-time, and once I become the new Sire, I'll change you and then we'll truly be able to start planning our *very* long future together."

The smile I plastered on my face was the best I could do and I hoped Christian bought it, because inside, I knew that was something I could never let happen. I was part demon and my blood would infect him, just as Meredith's had infected Terrance. I couldn't do that to Christian. Besides, the clan already vowed to hunt and kill any demons in the area. *Sucks to be me.*

Over the past four months I hadn't stopped thinking about Meredith's revelation that Dad and I were both demons. It was the reason she had gone after my mom. She'd wanted my dad for herself. It was pretty obvious my dad didn't have a clue, and that was a problem. I had no idea how I was going to learn anything about our heritage since I'd killed the only demon I'd ever encountered.

So many hurdles that would make it impossible for me to become Christian's consort. Yet out of necessity to remain hidden and safe, I was still living here with the clan. Evie had put me to work here at the club, so I actually had a real job and wasn't just a burden to them. I'd always been really good with numbers, so now I was in charge of keeping the books. Not that books were even necessary, since they could easily bite and use their sedative to manipulate anyone who would question them, like the liquor board or the IRS. But it was actually easier and more in-line with the clan's morals to run this business on the up-and-up. I certainly wasn't complaining, I finally had a real job.

When I'd first arrived, Justin and Christian had set me straight about the vampire facts that

Terrance had lied to me about. I'd learned vampires were actually really great people and nothing like how the history books or fables of old portrayed them. They only fed out of necessity, and always used the sedative that flowed from their fangs to make sure it never hurt their prey. All a vampire had to do was program their sedative to make their prey do and think whatever they wanted. So they always made it a pleasant experience, and then wiped their memories of the event. It's how vampires had been able to remain hidden from the world for centuries.

Almost a year ago, when I first found out vampires existed, I'd hoped to surprise Christian by going through the change and becoming a vampire like him so we could be together forever. But since Terrance was the one to tell me all about vampires and was unfortunately under Meredith's influence at the time, everything he told me had been a lie. There had been no way for him to make me a vampire as promised; that was something only a Sire could do. As I walked into the bathroom I called over my shoulder, "Do you have any idea when you'll become the new Sire?" *Please let it be a long time.*

"I'm not sure. My abilities are increasing but I think Evie wants to wait and see what other *talents* I develop before we do the Passing of Powers ritual. Honestly, I'm not even sure I'm really the one being triggered. It could all just be a big mistake."

Hope blossomed in my chest as I stared at myself in the foggy bathroom mirror. "What happens if it's not you?"

"I guess we just wait until someone else starts to show signs of being triggered."

Please let it not be him. The longer I had until a new Sire was triggered, the longer I had to figure out all this demon crap. One day very soon I was going to have to face my dad and get some answers. I didn't *think* he knew, but what if I was wrong and he'd known all along?

"I'm gonna hit the shower, but when I'm done...there's something I want to talk to you about."

CHAPTER TWO

Search

(Jeremy)

Today was the day I was going to find my little girl. I just knew it.

After her attack on Meredith, she and that boyfriend of hers, Christian, had gone into hiding. It hadn't taken me long to remember where he worked, but when I went to see the owner and asked if she'd seen them, the answer I'd gotten was, of course, no. I didn't believe her.

I'd thought about going to the police and asking them to get a search warrant, but since Meredith didn't press any charges and Rose was over eighteen, there really wasn't anything I could do except continue to look on my own. Besides, involving the police could be detrimental to us all since we'd covered up what had really happened that night.

I did find out from her college that she had completed her courses online and graduated on time, but they were unable to divulge any information as to where the computer's IP address was originating from without police involvement. Again, another dead end.

But today, I just had a feeling I was in for a lucky break. I had to take a trip back to Seela to go over some business accounts with my boss. After Meredith's recovery, I'd sold my home and moved to Masen to live with her. The decision wasn't easy, but it had been the best choice after my wife's death and Rose's attack on Meredith. I just couldn't stay in the home that carried all those horrible memories. It had been the place where I'd spent the happiest times of my life, but now it was just a constant reminder of everything I'd lost.

So I moved in with Meredith and we'd been blissfully happy for four months now. Her recovery had been almost miraculous according to the doctors. That type of injury usually would have been life-threatening, but Meredith barely had a scratch left on her, and she'd shocked all the therapists with how quickly she regained full mobility. She'd even gone back to work and so had I.

I was lucky enough to have moved my office to Masen, and instead of having to travel here every month or so, now I traveled back to Seela instead. Today was one of those days.

"Do you have everything?" Meredith bustled around the desk, gathering all the loose papers I had spread across it.

"Yes, honey. I have everything. I don't need those right now; they're for a different campaign." I was the Vice President of D&L Marketing and was headed to a meeting with my boss to go over my latest campaign proposal.

"Alright. I'll just stack them here then." She always made it a habit to keep my desk tidy for me. I wasn't sure if it was because she was just curious, or a neat freak who was still getting used to my presence in her life. I had tried to ask her about it once, and her response was, "Don't be silly. You're my destiny and I love having you here with me."

I was slowly starting to share her sentiment, but our relationship was something of a conundrum. I'd originally met Meredith when my wife, Loraine, was still alive, and the shock of how much the two looked alike had been intense: long blonde hair, a tall athletic body, and a killer smile. Then Loraine had died, and Meredith had really been there for me and we'd started dating.

I'd considered it a bit awkward to be dating a woman that reminded me of my dead wife, but at the time, it was exactly what I needed to help me deal with the pain. But when Rose found out, I was suddenly forced to look at the relationship in a whole new light. One that cast it as something that wasn't as bright and brilliant as I had made it out to be.

I tried to break it off with Meredith, but then the whole situation with Rose attacking her happened.

Her choosing not to press charges, but instead protect my daughter and me, well, that made me fall for her all over again.

"Are you going back to look for Rose at that club again?" Meredith asked, rousing me out of my stroll down memory lane.

"I was thinking about it. The owner said she hadn't seen either one of them since that night, but I don't believe her. I might just sit outside in my car instead of going in. Maybe that way I'll see something they weren't expecting me to see." I wiggled my eyebrows at her in an attempt to relay how sneaky and brilliant I thought my plan was.

"Well, just be careful. And call me when you get there. At least if I'm talking to you on the phone, I won't be worrying that something bad is happening to you." She straightened my tie, then wound her hands around the back of my neck and pulled me into a passionate kiss. "I just got you back and I never want to lose you again."

The feeling of Meredith's lips on mine and the sensual feel of her curves pressed against me had the potential to make me very late. This woman intoxicated me and I was so grateful to have her in my life during this difficult time, so I had to force myself out the door and into the garage.

I waved goodbye from the car as I pulled out of the driveway. The trip to Seela from Masen took about two hours, so that would give me plenty of time to think over my plan for tonight. The business meeting was going to be a breeze, same old same old, but a stakeout was something new to me. I certainly hoped it would lead me to Rose because as happy as Meredith and I were, I missed my baby girl.

* * * * *

(Meredith)

As soon as Jeremy waved goodbye and started to drive away, I grabbed the phone and dialed. "Have you had anymore reports of Rose and her vampire at The Rising Pit? Are they still there?"

"Yes, ma'am. According to our people, they're still there. Rose is now working for Evangeline as her bookkeeper."

Our people. I liked the sound of that. I came from a long line of human/demon descendants, but until recently, I'd only associated with my own family. But after some searching, I'd begun to find more demons in the area. I'd discreetly organized a few meetings to pull the demon families together. It was tricky since we'd spent our entire lives in hiding, but it was slowly working and it was nice to finally connect with people like me—with demons like me.

When I'd met Jeremy, he didn't have a clue that he was a demon, and he still didn't. I wasn't sure if I was going to tell him or not. I was afraid if he found out the truth about me, let alone himself, he'd start to question everything about our relationship again. And that was something I couldn't permit. Not after finally getting everything I'd worked so hard for.

When I discovered Jeremy was a demon, I'd made it my mission to seduce him in order to become pregnant and continue my pure demon bloodline. But I'd never expected to fall in love with him. Once I had, the only way to secure my life with him was to kill the one person who stood in my way...his wife. And now, having successfully separated Rose from her father, we'd finally been able to start our life together. So for now, I wouldn't tell him that he was a demon. At least not yet.

Besides, I wanted to spend more time with the other demons I'd met and see how they lived their lives and what of our histories they knew. A lot of demons were like Jeremy, clueless about their heritage, but every week, more and more demons were coming out of the woodwork and attending our little get-togethers. It was comforting. Especially since I knew it wouldn't be long until Rose and her boyfriend's clan found out that I was still alive. I knew they would be coming after me, and I'd have to be prepared. And the more demon "friends" I had, the better.

"I'm coming over. I have something I want to talk to you about."

CHAPTER THREE

Spy

(Christian)

Once again, I woke up realizing I was the luckiest vampire in the world. Rolling over in bed to find the love of my life, Rose, sleeping peacefully beside me was like waking up in heaven every night.

After gently brushing the hair out of her eyes, I leaned in and placed light kisses on her cheek before tiptoeing into our bathroom to shower. I needed to talk to Rose tonight. I wasn't looking forward to what I had to tell her, so I was happy for this brief time to myself to collect my thoughts.

After showering, I wrapped the towel around my waist and slowly crept back into the bedroom in case she was still sleeping. She wasn't. Instead I found her lying in bed with her hands tangled in her hair and a worried look on her face.

"Rose, are you okay?"

She sat up and a warm smile spread across her face while she looked at me standing there in nothing but a towel. If I hadn't been concerned over what she was worried about, I would have dropped the towel and proceeded to start our evening off in a much more delightful way, but with a crease to her brow, she pushed herself off our bed and wrapped her arms around me. "I was just thinking about everything that's happened. Terrance, Meredith, my dad. I...I just can't believe how much everything has changed."

I pulled back from the hug to press my lips to hers and then made sure to look her straight in the eye. I wanted her to know that she didn't have anything to worry about ever again. "I know, baby, but now you're living and working here full-time, and once I become the new Sire, I'll change you and then we'll truly be able to start planning our *very* long future together."

When I'd started to show signs of being triggered as the next Sire, I was completely skeptical. Actually...I was still pretty skeptical. I wasn't truly convinced that what was happening to me really meant I was the one, but in moments like these, I hoped it was true. Only a Sire had the ability to create another vampire, and the idea of being the one to turn Rose and to have her join me as my consort was euphoric.

She smiled at me and then headed towards the bathroom. As I walked towards my closet I heard her ask, "Do you have any idea when you'll become the new Sire?"

I was happy to hear the question because it meant she was thinking along the same lines as me. "I'm not sure. My abilities are increasing, but I think Evie wants to wait and see what other *talents* I develop before we do the Passing of Powers ritual. Honestly, I'm not even sure I'm really the one being triggered. It could all just be a big mistake." I didn't feel the need to hide my insecurities from Rose. We'd been through so much together, and I knew we'd face this together too.

"What happens if it's not you?" she called back.

After pulling on my jeans and slipping into a navy t-shirt, I shrugged. "I guess we just wait until someone else starts to show signs of being triggered."

I heard the water for the shower turn on and then Rose said, "I'm gonna hit the shower, but when I'm done...there's something I want to talk to you about."

I mulled over her words as I finished getting dressed, wondering what she could possibly want to talk to me about. I knew what I needed to tell her wasn't going to be easy for her to hear, but I thought it was something she needed to know. I hoped it would help her get some closure.

I was a little nervous about how she would react to the fact that Evie had recently sent Renard and Loni to spy on her father. Especially since what they'd found would come as a pretty big shock. Jeremy, Rose's dad, had sold their family home and moved away. I knew it was going to be devastating for Rose to hear, but she had a right to know.

After her attack on Meredith, Rose and I went into hiding here at The Rising Pit. A few weeks after the incident, however, Jeremy had come to the club looking for us. Evie turned him away, telling him she hadn't seen either of us since that night. He hadn't been back since.

At the time Evie had suggested that one of us bite him and use our sedative to make him forget, but Rose panicked at the idea. She'd said no matter how bad the memories her father had of her were, she just couldn't live with the idea that he wouldn't remember her at all. Evie tried to convince her we could wipe just the memories of Meredith and the attack, but Rose was adamant. She insisted that he needed to remember those things so he would be more willing to let her go.

Apparently her plan worked because he'd moved away completely, leaving the memories of what happened and any hopes of finding his daughter behind. I guess he realized his daughter was now a grown woman and there wasn't anything left for him to do but to move on.

It was a hard situation for everyone, and this conversation wasn't one I was looking forward to.

* * * * *

(Rose)

As I lathered my hair with my favorite honey and oat shampoo, I contemplated the best way to tell Christian that I wanted to go see my Dad. I knew he'd probably say no, that it was too risky, but honestly, I didn't care. It wasn't like he or any of his clan could stop me if I really wanted to go. I would just wait until they were all comatose during the day, and head out on my own.

I wasn't sure what I would say to my dad or how I would breach the demon subject, but I had to try. I needed to know why no one ever came after me for killing Meredith. Not that I wasn't happy about the fact, just confused. I needed to know once and for all if I was going to have to stay hidden forever.

I emerged from the bathroom in my terrycloth robe, towel drying my long blonde hair and found Christian pacing. "I've been thinking about it, and I want to go see my Dad." There. I'd said it. He stopped in his tracks and stared at me, then his hair and eyes started to drift.

"Did you hear me? I said I want to go see my dad."

"I heard you. But I have something I need to tell you."

"I don't care if you think it's a bad idea. He's my dad, and it's been four months since everything happened. If the cops haven't showed up yet, then I doubt they will. I need to know what he told them and I need to know if he's okay." I stomped back into the bathroom, threw my wet towel over the shower door, and then took a seat and started doing my makeup.

Christian entered the bathroom and stood behind me, placing his hands gently on my shoulders. I stopped applying my mascara and looked at him through our reflection in the mirror. "I didn't say it was a bad idea, but I have something to tell you which pertains to your dad that I think you need to hear first."

I pushed out of the seat and spun around to balance myself on the edge of the dressing table. "What? What do you need to tell me about my dad?" My grip tightened on the table, turning my knuckles white.

"Rose, your dad has moved. He sold the house and moved away."

CHAPTER FOUR

Ruse

(Rose)

It took me a moment to catch my breath. I'd heard what Christian said, but it just wasn't registering in my brain. There was no way my dad would have sold our home and moved away. I was born there, and every memory of my childhood revolved around us and that house.

"When? When did he move?" I couldn't get a grip on whether I was pissed or sad.

"We're not sure. Evie sent Renard and Loni to check on him a few weeks ago and they found the house with a sold sign in the yard and no one there."

I pushed off from my perch and began to walk out of the bathroom. Christian reached out to grab my arm but I quickly yanked it away. "Don't!"

Guess that settled it...I was pissed.

"How dare you keep this from me! You said that Evie sent them to check on him weeks ago and you just now decided to tell me?"

"I was going to tell you, but Evie wanted to try to gather more information, like where he moved to." Christian rushed to explain as he followed me out into the bedroom. "Unfortunately, we haven't found any forwarding address. Renard reported yesterday that he thinks your dad still works for the same place, even though most of his office has been cleared out."

I flopped down on the bed because I didn't trust my legs to keep me upright for much longer. As Christian continued speaking, I felt my head shaking *no* as if I was having an out of body experience. "If we could look around during the day it would be easier. We could use our sedative to force someone to tell us the information, but at night, running across someone who knew your dad has proven difficult." He knelt down in front of me and took my hands in his. "I'm sorry, Rose. I wasn't trying to keep it from you, I just wanted there to be more I could tell you when the time came."

I sat in silence and stared into Christian's eyes. They were drifting from caramel to dark brown and back again, along with his hair. It was obvious this was truly upsetting to him as well.

"I don't know what to say. I'm sad but also really mad. Can I just have some time alone?"

"Sure. But Rose, please know that I'm so sorry. Sorry for not telling you before, and sorry it happened in the first place." He kissed my hands, placed them back in my lap, and then strolled out of the room, shutting the door behind him.

I sat there stunned, thinking back to when my dad had come looking for me shortly after I'd gone into hiding. It'd made me feel good to know that after everything, he still wanted me in his life.

At the time, Evie suggested that they bite him and make him forget everything, but I just couldn't allow that to happen. Not for the obvious reasons I gave them of course, but because if they bit him they'd become infected with his demon blood. Skating around that had been a little tricky, but I convinced them not to bite him, and instead just tell him that Christian and I hadn't been back to the bar since that night.

It hurt to know my ruse had worked so well, and that my dad had really given up on me. I knew I had no right to feel hurt by his actions; in his eyes I was a murderer and a runaway. Why did I expect him to care? This was exactly what I hoped would happen. But at the time, I also thought I would soon be a vampire, and would need to cut all ties because of it. But instead, that dream had been shattered. My heart still hurt over losing my mom, and now being faced with having to live a mortal life without Christian or my father...I suddenly felt very alone.

I curled up on the bed, drew the covers around me, and did the only thing I could do: cry myself back to sleep.

* * * * *

(Christian)

As I walked down the white tiled hall of our secure lair, which was located deep beneath The Rising Pit, I realized I wasn't ready to face everyone just yet. Usually, once everyone awoke for the night, we'd all meet upstairs and head out together to feed before opening the club for business. But tonight...I just couldn't deal with everyone questioning my bad mood. I hadn't stopped drifting yet so they would immediately know something was wrong. Rose and I had been so happy since she moved in, and honestly, I was feeling a little embarrassed to admit to everyone that we seemed to be having our first real fight.

So, instead of heading for the spiral staircase that led up and out into the club from underneath the stage, I took the turn at the end of the hall which led to the area where the blood bags were kept. I would have to make do with cold blood tonight if I wanted to avoid everyone for a little while longer.

"Hey, what are you doing down here?" Bobby asked as I entered the room.

So much for that plan. "Nothing. What are you doing here?"

"It's my turn to give Terrance his pity meal." Evie had stocked the room with blood bags the night after Terrance had been chained up. Even though he had done some pretty bad things, she would never let him starve, so each night we took turns taking him his blood.

I turned around and started to head back to my room, but felt Bobby follow me out the door. "So tell me. What *are* you doing down here? I can tell you're upset. Did Rose stop putting out?" He chuckled, which was normal for Bobby...make light of every situation.

It didn't surprise me Bobby picked up on the fact that I was upset. He would have known even if I hadn't been drifting. Best friends always had a way of knowing when something was wrong, and Bobby and I had been best friends since the moment I'd saved him and asked that he be turned.

It was 1613, and we were in England to attend the marriage festivities of Frederick V and Princess Elizabeth, which included performances of six of

Shakespeare's plays. Bobby had been one of the actors.

After one of the shows, the actors were drinking and apparently there had been a scuffle and Bobby ended up getting shot through the chest. I'd been out walking, looking for someone to feed on, when I'd smelled the blood. They had dumped his body in the river on the edge of the grounds. He was barely alive, but just enough that Evangeline was able to save him. We'd been best friends ever since.

"I just told Rose about her dad moving and she didn't take it very well."

I prepared myself for his snide comment, but for once it didn't come. Our footsteps echoed in the hall as we continued to walk in silence towards Terrance's cell.

We didn't bother to stop for chit chat; Bobby just tossed the blood bag into Terrance's lap and kept walking, but then I heard something that stopped me dead in my tracks. "I swear I'm gonna kill that bitch."

Thankfully, I could now tell the difference when my *skills* flared up, allowing me to hear someone's thoughts. Before I just thought they'd been whispering something under their breath, but this was definitely one of Terrance's thoughts, and if it was about Rose... "What did you just think? You swear you're gonna kill who? I promise you Terrance, if you are talking about Rose, I'll have Evie kill you tonight!"

He sat there staring at me while the muscle in his jaw ticked at an annoying pace. "I wasn't thinking about Rose. I was thinking about Meredith. The demon bitch who did this to me."

Bobby looked at me with a frown on his face, while I was stunned into silence. This shouldn't be possible. Meredith's blood had infected Terrance, causing all memories of her to become fuzzy, ultimately hiding her involvement, even to him. He'd never been able to think clearly about her before, and shouldn't be able to think about her now, let alone contemplate killing her. Something was happening to him.

As I looked closer, I noticed his hair wasn't quite as dark and his eyes seemed slightly lighter too. *My god, could he actually be drifting back?* "Bobby, go get Evie. Now!"

CHAPTER FIVE

Possibility

(Rose)

I woke up in Christian's bed...our bed, and immediately wanted to be somewhere else. I was shocked at the intensity of my feelings. Being with Christian had been all I'd wanted for the past year, but now...I just felt so stifled. I knew it was stemming from finding out about Dad selling our family home, but learning that had apparently opened a floodgate of emotions which were now threatening to overwhelm me.

Maybe I could find Dad and smooth things over with him so we could live together again. Or maybe Jillian and I could get that apartment together like she wanted. I just knew that since becoming a vampire was no longer an option, I needed to come up with a new plan.

I knew it was something that would take some time to figure out, and luckily time was on my side. As Christian had pointed out, their clan was in transition. They currently didn't have a Sire who could change me, and right now, that was a very good thing.

I knew Christian wasn't sure if he was truly the next in-line, but regardless of who the new Sire ended up being, it wouldn't matter. I'd never become a vampire and I wasn't sure how I was going to convince Christian to let me go without telling him the truth. But the fight we just had presented me with a pretty good opportunity.

As much as it hurt me to do it, I would continue to act betrayed that he didn't tell me about my father sooner and slowly begin to pull away. But first, I had to find my dad. I needed to know if I was a wanted fugitive and how he really felt about everything that had happened. Maybe after leaving The Rising Pit I could move back in with him and things could go back to normal. The problem was, I now had no idea where to begin my search.

My self-pity party continued as I got up to finish getting ready. I was just so mad, hurt, and confused. A year ago, I had a plan that would allow me to live forever with the man I loved—and now everything was ruined. I wallowed in everything I was feeling as I finished my makeup. Then I threw on a pair of jeans, a purple tank top, and slid into my flip-flops before flopping back down on the bed.

I grabbed my new cell phone and prepared to call Jillian. It was a risk, but it also seemed like the most logical thing to do. My parents had been friends with her parents for so long, and I didn't think my Dad would have left town without telling them where he went.

"Jillian? It's Rose. Please don't hang up." I was happy that she picked up at all since she wouldn't have recognized my new number. Christian had insisted I get a new phone when we'd gone into hiding.

"Hang up? Are you fucking kidding me? I've been worried sick about you! Where the hell are you?"

I almost started crying at the sound of her voice and the fact that she was worried about me. I wasn't sure how any of my friends would feel about me since I'd disappeared. "I'm sorry, I can't tell you where I am, but please know I'm okay. How are you? How have things been since I...left?"

"Oh my god, Rose, it's been crazy. First, you just disappear off the face of the earth, and then your dad up and sells your house to move to Masen and live with that woman. It's just been crazy. My parents are freaking out."

"Wait. What? Masen? What woman?"

"That Meredith bitch he was seeing. After you left, they moved to Masen together. Are you saying you haven't even talked to your dad this whole time?"

Oh my god, no! She can't be alive and still with my dad. I dropped the phone and started to hyperventilate. This couldn't be happening. How the hell could she still be alive?

Jillian's voice echoed out of my phone. "Rose, are you still there? Rose?"

Once the adrenaline kicked in, I grabbed my phone again. "Jillian, you can't tell anyone I called, okay?"

"What? Why? Rose, why can't you tell me what's going on? Your dad has been looking for you and I miss you too. Where are you?"

With this new development, it was so important no one knew I'd contacted Jillian that I did the unthinkable...I threatened my best friend. "Jillian, I'm not kidding. You can't tell anyone I called. If you do, I'll kill you!"

Her loud exhale told me how offended she was, but right now I didn't care. I knew it made me seem like a real asshole, but I just couldn't risk anyone finding out that I'd contacted her. They'd start poking around again, looking for me, and that was something I couldn't risk. Besides, the urgency I felt to get to Christian and tell him that we still had a demon problem to deal with, left me with no time to explain. Jillian was just going to have to continue to think I'd lost my mind.

I didn't wait for her response; I simply hung up and headed for the door. I couldn't believe Meredith was still alive and now had my dad within her reach 24/7.

CHAPTER SIX

Recruiting

(Meredith)

It didn't take me long to reach Damien's house. He only lived about ten miles away. He was the first demon I ran across after starting my search. He and his family had lived in the area for seventy-five years, and he told me I was the first demon outside their immediate family they'd ever met. We became fast friends. He was single and about the same age as Jeremy and I. He spent a lot of time with his cousins and started bringing them to our meetings. At this point, we had about twenty demons who showed up to our meetings on a regular basis. I was hoping that number would continue to grow.

As we made our way to the living room, he asked, "Hey, so what did you need to talk to me about that couldn't wait until this week's meeting?"

"I wanted to see how familiar you are with some of the ancient ways. I have something I want to share with the group, but wanted to run it by you first." I sat on the thread bare couch and waited for his response.

I could tell by the way he puffed up his chest he felt privileged that I'd chosen to share this information with him before anyone else. I didn't care how he felt as long as he was willing to do what I wanted. It wasn't because I met him first that I chose to share this information with him, but instead because after a little background check, he wasn't exactly the upstanding citizen he led everyone to believe. I was pretty sure he would be a power hungry demon who'd revel in increasing his powers. Time to test my theory.

"Well, my abuela use to tell me some pretty freaky stories. Why? What exactly did you want to know?"

"Well, did you know that our demon ancestors actually drank human blood?"

"Yeah. She told me that and how they thought it would extend their life because they were ingesting another person's essence or some crazy shit like that."

Time to drop the bombshell. "It's not crazy shit. It works. It's happened to me."

His eyes nearly popped out of his head but at least he didn't run off screaming.

"I was injured recently, and because I chose to drink human blood to test the theory of our ancestors, I healed almost instantly." I waited to gauge his response before continuing. He was still staring at me but the glint in his eye was enough to tell me that he was extremely interested in what I had to say. "I also found that by drinking human blood, I gained inhuman amounts of strength."

Suddenly serious, he stood. "Show me."

I stood up from the couch and then picked it up...with one hand.

"Believe me?"

The evil grin that spread across Damien's face was the last piece of confirmation I needed to know I'd chosen the right guy. "Yes. Now who do we have to kill to get some fresh human blood?"

"That's exactly the question I hoped you'd ask."

We spent the next two hours going over everything I'd learned from my experience with the vampires and from killing Loraine. We talked about who else he thought would be willing to join us in enhancing our demon powers and our new quest for immortal life. He didn't have a clue about the vampires, but was now excited to start drinking human blood so he would be ready to take them on.

This was going perfectly. My recruiting had officially begun.

* * * * *

(Jeremy)

The afternoon spent in my meeting flew by. It was now dusk and I was headed to The Rising Pit. I still had a feeling that I would catch a lucky break tonight. I really hoped I was right; it had been too long since I'd seen my daughter. When the accident happened everything had been so chaotic. I hadn't been in my right mind and I just sat there watching as she ran out of my life. But now that Meredith had recovered and we'd become settled in our new life together, it was time I found out exactly why Rose had attacked her in the first place.

Whenever I asked Meredith to give me details about that night, she would only say that her memories were too foggy and that she just couldn't remember. All she recalled was that she'd come over late to talk to me and had apparently startled Rose and Christian who had seemed to be fighting. When she tried to step in, Rose went ballistic, yelling things about Meredith killing her mom and other ridiculous stuff.

That didn't sound like my Rose, but I saw her attack Meredith with my own eyes and watched as she fled with her boyfriend. At this point, I wasn't really sure I knew anything about my daughter anymore.

I eased my Lexus into the very farthest parking spot I could find. It was in the very back corner of the club's lot and didn't have any lights surrounding it. So far I was pretty pleased with my sleuthing skills.

I sat there for about twenty minutes before the club's front door opened and out walked Evangeline with a few members of her staff, but unfortunately, neither Rose nor Christian were amongst them. I blew out the breath I was holding only to have all of them snap their heads in my direction. I knew they couldn't see me way back here but I unconsciously slouched down in my seat because it felt as if they were looking right at me. It was odd. I watched as Evangeline whispered something into one of the guy's ears and then he walked back into the club as the rest of them headed off in a different direction.

I checked my watch and realized I would only have another thirty minutes to spy before I needed to hit the road in order to make it home in time for dinner. It looked like my lucky break wasn't going to happen after all.

CHAPTER SEVEN

Alive

(Rose)

The moment I entered the hallway I heard voices in the direction of Terrance's cell. I picked up my pace, anxious to see what the commotion was about, but especially because I was desperate to reach Christian and tell him that Meredith was still alive.

"Are you sure he's remembering her and not just going off the things he's heard us saying about her?" I heard Evie ask.

"No, he seems to be remembering specific things about her. I've been able to pick up on certain thoughts and they really are about Meredith," Christian said.

As I grabbed Christian's arm and spun him towards me, the worried look on his face was enough to stop me from blurting out what I'd originally come to say. "What's going on? Why are you talking about Meredith?"

"Terrance has started to remember things about Meredith. Somehow the thoughts are breaking through and he's really pissed about how she manipulated him." Christian eased his arm around me as he continued. "I heard some of his internal thoughts when I was walking by earlier, and it appears he's starting to drift back. We're just trying to figure out how any of this is even possible."

"Well, I know one person we could talk to to find out." Everyone looked at me as if I'd sprouted another head. "Meredith. I just found out she's still alive."

Christian's mouth dropped open and Evie stumbled back a step, while Terrance just let out a roar that sent goose bumps racing up my arms.

They were right...he did sound pissed.

"I'll kill that bitch for what she did to me. She caused me to lose the one and only thing I've cared about in over three-hundred years!" His chains rattled as he strained against them.

"How do you know this?" Evie asked.

I took a shaky breath then answered. "I called Jillian. She told me my dad sold our house and moved to Masen to live with Meredith. Apparently, being a demon has some perks."

"I can't believe this. If she's still out there, then what's going to stop her from coming after Rose, or from infecting another vampire in the area to do her dirty work? We have to find her and kill her!" Christian was drifting so fast that it was making me dizzy. Everyone else's emotions were starting to show as well. Seeing Evie with dark hair and an angry look on her face had me making a mental note to never piss her off.

"How are we going to kill her if she has super-healing abilities and lord knows what else? We know nothing about the demons except that they're really strong and fast, and we can't bite them because we'll become infected. We're flying blind here." Bobby, for once, was the voice of reason.

Evie's hair and eyes evened out as she stepped into the center of our little crowd. "Alright. Everyone just sit tight. Terrance, I'm sorry, but even though you're showing signs of breaking through whatever hold Meredith had on you, we just don't know enough to let you out yet. Christian, you and Rose stay here. I won't chance you running into Meredith until we come up with a plan. The rest of us need to go out and feed, but once the club's open tonight, I'm going to call Balam again to see if he can provide us with some more information."

Terrance slid down the wall and sat on the floor as the rest of the clan headed for the stairs.

"Do you want to go up and order some food?" Christian asked.

"Sure." I reached for his hand but immediately regretted it when a smile spread across his face. I couldn't let him think we were making up. Even with this new development, things hadn't changed for me. I was going to have to stick to my guns.

I pulled my hand out of his and started up the stairs, trying to think of a way to handle all of this. Currently...I was coming up blank.

Sounding defeated, Christian asked, "What would you like for dinner, Rose?"

"Chinese sounds fine."

After emerging from below the stage, I sat down at one of the tables as Evie, Dax, Bobby, Tori, and Dom left the club to go feed, while

Renard and Loni both took seats at the bar. Christian had just pulled out his cell to place our order when Bobby suddenly walked back through the door. Using his vampire speed, he was at Renard and Loni's side in a split second.

"Excuse me a second, I need to see what's going on." I watched Christian make his way over to them. I strained my ears, trying to hear what was happening. I wondered what drama was unfolding now.

I hadn't really gotten to know much about the couple yet, except that Renard was originally from England and that's where they'd taken their honeymoon so he could show his cute American wife all the places he frequented as a human.

They both had a punk-rocker look about them. Renard's hair was a dirty blonde, smooth yet spiky at the same time. Loni had a short, edgy cut of blonde hair that was tipped in black. No one was sure why her hair had drifted like that when she was turned, but Evie assumed it was because she witnessed her sister being killed when she was a little girl. By the time she was turned, it was a distant memory, but Evie thought it was possible the memory still remained buried deep within her psyche. All I knew was that she was really sweet and pretty badass. She was the only female security guard on the staff. Now with Meredith being back in the picture, I was really glad they were both here and had Christian's back.

* * * * *

(Christian)

"What's going on?" I asked.

"We just caught Rose's dad staked out in his car at the back of the parking lot. Evie wants Renard and Loni to follow him back to Masen so we can find out where Meredith is. It's a pretty lucky break. What are the odds he'd show up tonight after all this time?"

"Yeah, a lucky break." I knew I'd started drifting again as I walked back to Rose. How was I going to tell her that her dad was just outside and expect her not to go to him?

"So, what's up? What was that all about?" she asked.

"Let me order you some dinner first, and then we can talk about everything." I needed to allow as much time to pass as possible so hopefully her father would be long gone by the time I broke the news.

She crossed her arms and sat back in her chair. "Alright. But I'm not sure how much there is to talk about. It's obvious now why no one ever came after me for killing Meredith...because I didn't kill her. And as far as my dad is concerned, he made his choice to leave behind all memories of me and my mother to go be with her, so I don't see that there's really anything to talk about at all." The tears shining in her eyes broke my heart, and my will.

"I think there's a lot we need to talk about. Like how Meredith could somehow be controlling him like she was controlling Terrance. She could have forced him to sell the house and move to Masen with her; we really don't know. Until Evie gets some more information from Balam, I think we should just stay out of sight and off her radar, and unfortunately that means no more phone calls. But Rose, you should know, your dad still loves you and hasn't stopped looking for you. He hasn't left you behind. As a matter of fact, he was just sitting outside in his car probably hoping to catch a glimpse of you."

I knew I'd said the wrong thing when she stood up so fast that her chair slammed to the floor.

"Christian! My dad was just here and you didn't tell me?"

"Rose, please. I literally *just* found out."

It was clear she was too mad to hear anything else I had to say because she continued her rant without skipping a beat. "And how dare you try to tell me who I can or can't call? It's a damn good thing I did call Jillian, otherwise we wouldn't even know about Meredith!" She stomped towards the stairs but stopped before heading down. "Your whole clan is the same way. You think you all have the best ideas about what to do, but really...you guys don't have a clue about what's happening around here or how to handle any of it!"

I slammed my fist into the table, shredding it to splinters. Bobby, Renard, and Loni's heads were swiveling between me and a retreating Rose. So much for keeping our fight under wraps. This whole situation was out of control and as much as I wanted to race after Rose and try to smooth things over, I couldn't...because she was right. We didn't have a clue as to what to do next. So until Evie had some more information and told us what the plan was, I was just going to have to let Rose cool off alone. I was tired of disappointing her.

CHAPTER EIGHT

Success

(Meredith)

Damien and I were crouched around a homeless man in the alley behind the Salvation Army. The stench of sweat and garbage was almost too much for me to handle. But, I'd been so happy with the success of our conversation, we'd decided to put our theory to the test right away.

I'd gone over the plan again and again on our way over, and Damien was content with letting me start the process. I sunk my teeth into the man's neck, and with only a little pressure had my first taste of warm blood since I'd killed Loraine. It was heaven.

My body was filled with a rush of strength and my heart picked up its pace as the man's essence filled my soul.

"Enough, Meredith. My turn," Damien demanded. I was so caught up in the sensation I didn't realize I'd fed longer than expected.

"I'm sorry, you're right. Here." I tossed him the man's body and watched as he sank his teeth in the already open wounds on his neck. I was pleased but surprised he didn't show any signs of hesitating.

Watching the actual process and effect the human blood had on him was astonishing. It was almost as if Damien grew taller and wider right before me. The flare of red in his eyes signaled just how much he was enjoying the effects of the blood.

Breathing heavily and with crimson coating his mouth, Damien pulled away from the man and dropped his dead body to the ground. "It's working. I can feel it happening just like you said."

"I told you; you can trust me. Now that we know how to get stronger and extend our lives, I think it's time we started to look for others who'd do the same. Because once the vampires in Seela find out I'm still alive, they're going to come after me. The more demons we have ready to fight, the better our chances will be."

"I know a handful of people in my family that may be willing to join us, but the majority will be appalled by what we're doing."

"What if we don't tell them? What if we put some blood in the drinks at the next meeting, and little by little feed them the essence that will make them stronger? Once they realize they are being affected, they won't want to stop."

His sly smile told me he agreed with my plan. "You're brilliant. And gorgeous." In the next second I was being slammed against the hard brick wall. "I want you Meredith. I want you right here, right now." I knew he was reacting to the high of the human blood in our veins, but I loved Jeremy and I wanted him to be the father of my baby...not Damien.

"Damien, back the fuck off!" I shoved him off of me and straightened my shirt. I was stronger than him and wasn't worried about stopping his advance. "I'm flattered, but there's no way in hell I'm sleeping with you, and if you pull that shit again, I'll have your balls on a platter before you can blink. I need someone I can count on as my second, not someone whose emotions and feelings are going be an issue. Can I count on you or should I start looking for someone else?"

"I'm sorry. I think I'm just overwhelmed by the blood in my system. Please accept my apology. Of course you can count on me." He lowered his head as we made our way out of the dark alley and back to the car.

"Good. I have to get home, but let's meet tomorrow night so we can gather some more 'donors' to prepare for the next meeting."

The look on Damien's face confirmed he was on board with my plan. The anticipation of killing and drinking another human's blood as soon as tomorrow had his eyes glowing red, and a gluttonous smile was plastered on his face. "That sounds perfect!"

* * * * *

(Jeremy)

I wasn't sure, but I thought I was being followed as I headed back towards Masen. The blue SUV had been on me since I'd left The Rising Pit.

Evangeline and the rest of her crew—minus the guy who disappeared back inside—hadn't come back before I left, but as I pulled onto the freeway and pointed my car towards home, this truck had been behind me. *Damn, I'm getting paranoid again.*

During the two hour drive from Seela to Masen, I tested my theory. I changed lanes, sped up and slowed down, and finally began to relax when I no longer saw the truck behind me. I pulled out my cell to give Meredith a heads up that I was almost home. "Hi, honey, I'm almost to the edge of town. Did you eat already or do I need to pick something up for us?"

"I would love some pizza if you're up for it. I can call Giovanni's and have it ready for pickup if you'd like."

Hearing her voice settled my nerves. After striking out on my stakeout, the idea of a romantic evening with Meredith was just what I needed. "Pizza and wine. That sounds perfect, babe. I'll be there in thirty minutes."

CHAPTER NINE

Trigger

(Evie)

Once Renard and Loni were on their way to
Masen to gather intel on Jeremy and Meredith,
Dax and the others opened the club as I settled in
my office and prepared to call my Sire once again.

I asked Christian to join me so he could relay
the details of exactly what happened with Terrance
if necessary.

Balam answered on the second ring, obviously
recognizing my number from the caller id.
"Evangeline. What's wrong? I didn't expect to hear
from you again so soon."

"I'm sorry to bother you again, Sire, but our
situation is far from over and there have been
some developments that are causing even more
confusion."

"What developments, jovencita?" It was hard for him not to speak in his native tongue, but he knew that I'd stopped speaking Spanish a very long time ago. But he still couldn't resist calling me by the nickname he'd labeled me with so long ago..."young one."

A small burst of laughter escaped me at the oddity of being called "young one." Me, a twelve-hundred year old vampire. But it did solidify just how ancient Balam truly was. I hoped being one of the original Mayan people would lend itself to him possessing some valuable information once again.

"The demon is still alive and my vampire son, Terrance, has shown signs of drifting back to normal. I was hoping you might have an idea as to how that's even possible. I know the rule is to deliver the true death to any vampire who's drifted permanently dark, but if he's drifting back, I think we need to make an exception to the rule." The speed of my explanation was apparently enough of a trigger for Balam to understand how panicked I truly was.

"Evangeline, calm down. After we last spoke I contacted the other elders and we've discussed your situation at length. I think you're right; ending Terrance would be a mistake. He's the first vampire to ever go through something like this and come out of it alive. Our lack of information in the past has led to some unfortunate deaths, but now that we know demons are responsible for the few cases in which vampires drifted permanently dark, this is the perfect opportunity to study Terrance and his reactions and maybe find a solution to the problem through his experience."

Relieved, I closed my eyes and took a deep breath as I sunk into my leather chair. I was so happy Terrance would be allowed to live. Christian remained seated on the opposite side of my desk, watching me intently as he listened with his heightened hearing as Balam continued.

"I think one of the reasons Terrance has started drifting back is due to the lack of demon blood being introduced into his system. He hasn't fed from the demon in months, so it would make sense that her blood would work its way out of his system. Our rule of delivering the true death was something that Yum Camil established before my time and has always prompted us to end our affected brethren before they ever had a chance to recover."

I hoped Balam was right, as this would mean that Terrance would soon drift back to normal and fully become part of our clan once more. My hopes were quickly dashed as Balam spoke again.

"You are not going to be able to let Terrance free because even though the demon blood no longer poisons his system, we are not sure how the mind bond that was forged will be affected. Just because he's not feeding from her doesn't mean she couldn't still have the ability to control him."

Damn! That was really bad news. Christian's eyes and hair were almost black as he shook his head. I knew how upset he was and exactly what he was thinking. Killing her and every other demon we could find was going to be our only choice.

"Balam, do you and the elders have any ideas on how we actually kill a demon?"

"Let me contact the elders once more and I will call you in a couple of days. The stories of our origins and the ancient demon culture are scarce, but I'm sure through our combined knowledge we'll be able to pinpoint the details you'll need to put an end to this nightmare."

I thanked my Sire and hung up the phone. This was going to be a long couple of days.

"Do you think they have a chance of uncovering the information we need to destroy her?" The skepticism in Christian's voice proved he didn't think so.

"I'm not sure. We're facing something new for the first time in all of vampire history, and that means there are a lot of unknowns. Even Balam has never been through something like this. But I trust him to do everything he can to help us find the answer." With that, I pushed out of my chair and headed to find Dax. I knew my consort would want to know everything I'd just learned. Christian's hand on my shoulder stopped me just as I reached the door.

"Rose and I had a fight. She's mad at me for not telling her about her dad moving when we first found out. And now, with Meredith being alive, I think she's even more determined to contact her dad to find out what's going on. She's lost faith that we'll be able to control the situation and I think she's losing faith in our relationship too. I don't know what to do."

The crestfallen look on his face had my heart breaking. This was Christian's first serious relationship in six-hundred years. "I'm so sorry, Christian, but try to understand. Rose has lost her entire family, and is now being forced to live with a bunch of vampires who can only interact with her at night. She must be feeling pretty alone, and then to find out we've been keeping things from her...you must see how that could be very upsetting."

"I do. And I'm sorry I didn't tell her sooner. You said that you wanted to gain more information first, and at the time I agreed with you, but I think we made a mistake. We're going to have to trust Rose more. Especially since once I become the new Sire, she'll be my consort forever.

I don't want any animosity between us right from the start."

"You're right. We do need to trust her more, but keep in mind, Christian, she's still human. Their emotions can make them do irrational things."

"Like run straight into the waiting arms of a demon because she misses her dad?" Christian asked.

"Exactly. And honestly, you do realize we have no way of stopping her from leaving during the day, don't you? Unless you plan to bite and use your sedative on a human, there's no other way to keep tabs on her while we sleep."

"I thought about that, and even though it will push her further away if she ever finds out, I feel like she's leaving me no choice. I'm so terrified of what Meredith will do to her if she gets the chance. And Rose's fear for her father's safety is likely to push her straight into Meredith's grasp."

"Take tonight and think things over. If you want to use a human to guard her during the day, I know the perfect one. Just let me know what you decide."

* * * * *

(Christian)

I left Evie's office and took a trip around the club, for once doing my job instead of focusing on Rose. Well, almost. I needed time to think on how best to approach Rose with my apology...and my demands.

There was no way I could risk her running to her father, only to fall prey to Meredith's scheme, whatever it was. I knew before I even reached the upper level of the club that I was going to take

Evie up on her offer. I had to have someone

who'd be able to watch over Rose while I was

comatose. I would bite this human, and program

my sedative to turn him into her bodyguard. He

would keep tabs on her, and if necessary, do

anything and everything to protect her. I didn't

think it was something Rose would be upset

about–people get body guards all the time...right?

CHAPTER TEN

It was Over

(Rose)

I slammed the door to our room so hard I thought it would fly off its hinges. I couldn't believe my dad had just been here and they had all kept me from going to him. What harm could it have done if he was alone? I hadn't killed Meredith, so it wasn't like I needed to worry about being chased by the cops any more, and talking to my dad might have given us a better idea about what was happening with her. Then again, maybe Christian was right. Maybe she was controlling my dad like she controlled Terrance. Who knew? And even if she wasn't controlling him, I'm sure she was probably keeping tabs on him as a way to find and probably kill me.

I threw myself onto the bed and buried my face in the pink covered feather pillow. The familiar scent and texture had my eyes filling with tears. It was the pillow I'd had in my old bedroom. The pillow my mom and I picked out together when we redid my bedroom after our painting project all those months ago. *Months?* It felt like years.

Shortly after Christian and I had gone into hiding, I was so sad about having to leave my home that I longed for something to remind me of my old life. So, Christian, without Evie's knowledge, snuck back into my house and grabbed some of my clothes and a few small things that wouldn't be missed from my room, including my pillow. He hadn't run into my dad or anyone else, and I was so grateful to have some of my things that I never even considered the risk.

Yes, we'd thought Meredith was dead at the time, but he could have run into her and if he'd bitten her, he would have drifted dark and been under her control, just like Terrance. Which was the same thing that would happen if he bit me. What a nightmare this had become.

I sat up, resolute in my decision. I would put an end to this here and now. I grabbed the box of my things that was stashed under the bed and found my special stationary and pen. I would write Christian a letter telling him it was over. I had to get out of this situation while I had a good reason, and right now, with how mad I was and all the "fighting" we'd been doing, it was the perfect time.

I'd just finished my letter when I heard footsteps outside the door. I watched as the knob slowly turned and Christian called out, "Rose, are you in there?"

I quickly crumpled the paper, threw it into the box, and pushed the whole thing back under the bed. I simply wasn't ready to give it to him just yet. I needed to know what he and Evie found out from Balam, and I figured I could always rewrite it and give it to him later. Or possibly leave it on the bed during the day while he slept, taking the coward's way out.

"I'm here."

His head was hanging low as he made his way to join me on the bed. "I'm sorry" was all he said.

I sat in silence, considering the best way to handle this. I couldn't forgive him like I wanted to, throwing my arms around his neck and kissing him until we ended up having make-up sex. No, I had to keep my shields in place. He had to believe that I was still mad, or else he'd dig for the real reason I was leaving. A reason I could never reveal.

"I hate fighting with you, Rose. Can we please talk this through? I already explained I didn't tell you about your dad moving because Evie wanted to gather more information first, but I admit that was a mistake. And about what just happened upstairs, I honestly just found out about your dad being here right before I told you, I swear."

"I believe you. But Christian, the problem is...I'm starting to feel like a prisoner here. I should've been happy to find out that I'm not a wanted murderer, but instead, I still have to remain here, hidden and scared, because the woman I *tried* to kill is still alive and wants me dead. I love you and I appreciate Evie taking me in and everyone accepting me, but I miss my friends and my dad. This whole situation has been twisted around, and I'm just not sure if staying here is right for me anymore."

The shocked look on his face was enough to make me want to take everything back. I hated hurting him. But if things went back to the way there were, then he would think I was still planning to become his consort, and that was something that could never happen. At least this way I was protecting him from being *truly* hurt.

"Rose, I know you're mad, and I certainly don't want you to feel like a prisoner here, but you have to understand that you and I remaining under wraps is for your own safety. I wish I was the new Sire already so I could just change you into a vampire, and then we wouldn't have to worry about this anymore. Meredith couldn't hurt you once you were like me."

I pushed off the bed and spun around to face him. "How can you say that? You guys are in more danger from Meredith than I am. If you bite her, you'll become infected and then she'll be able to control you. Have you forgotten that? At least with me, the *human*, all she can do is kill me. I'd rather be dead than be controlled."

"Dammit, Rose!" Christian flew across the room and had me by the arms in the next second. "No, I haven't forgotten any of what's happened, but don't you dare say stuff like that. Don't you dare say you'd rather be dead! I can't bear to hear it." He released me and ran his hand through his rapidly drifting hair. "I know vampires can't bite her, but soon we'll have the information we need to kill her. If you were a vampire, you'd be strong enough to stand against her. That's all I meant."

I hated putting him through this. I almost meant what I'd said. I'd rather be dead, if only to avoid causing him pain. "Christian, I'm sorry this is hard to hear, but I'm going to reach out to my dad and find out what's going on very soon. There's really nothing you can do to stop me, and it upsets me you'd even want to try. Don't you want to know what's up with Meredith?"

Christian was breathing heavy and he hadn't stopped drifting, but I didn't expect the menace in his voice when he said, "Evie already sent Renard and Loni to check things out with your dad and the demon. We should know their whereabouts by tomorrow. But Rose...you're wrong if you think there's nothing I can do to stop you."

CHAPTER ELEVEN

Make This Work

(Meredith)

After spending a perfect evening with Jeremy, eating pizza, drinking wine, and making love, I took the next day off from work, faking a cold. I had too much to do to prepare for the next demon meeting.

Damien and I were going to meet in an hour to check out the prospects for tonight's bloodletting. He'd been disappointed when I told him we wouldn't be able to continue drinking and draining our victims to death. No, we had to start draining and storing it so it could be introduced to the other demons at the meetings as planned, though killing the *donors* was still the ultimate end to the process.

"I'll be there in an hour. Are the workers still in the area?" I asked.

"Yes. They're taking a lunch break now, but once the horn sounds, they branch off again and head to their designated areas. There's one section way in the back and only two workers are assigned there. It's perfect."

"I'll decide if it's perfect once I'm there. I'm leaving now."

Damien had found what he thought was the perfect place to obtain some of our victims. There was a logging facility outside of town that had recently hired a large crew of Labor Ready employees. He figured it would be the ideal situation since there were so many new faces; it was likely that no one would miss the men we took.

Honestly, I didn't care if they were missed or not, as long as I got what I needed and we didn't leave any evidence behind. I wasn't stupid and had recently bought a bundle of gloves so our fingerprints wouldn't be found in the area. We'd have to knock these men out and transport them to a secure location before draining them.

When Damien first told me his plan, I looked up the area on the computer and found there was an abandoned hunting shack just a quarter mile from the location. I figured with my demon speed, it wouldn't take me long to transport the men there to meet their death. I had everything we needed to make it look like they wandered off to get high and met their end by way of a wild animal. I was sure we could make this work.

As I gathered the last of my supplies and stuffed them in my oversized purse, I glanced out the kitchen window and noticed a blue SUV parked across the street. I couldn't recall if it had been there last night, but I'd lived here long enough to notice a strange car in the vicinity. I looked closer but didn't see anyone in the vehicle so I made a mental note to check and see if it was still there when I came home tonight.

I eased into my BMW, excited about starting this next phase of my plan and sped towards my meeting with Damien.

* * * * *

(Renard)

It didn't take long for Jeremy to notice that he was being tailed, so I backed off and let him think he lost us. Evie had been very specific with her instructions. We were to follow him and find out where he and Meredith lived, but were not to engage either of them.

After tailing him to some pizza joint and the liquor store, where he purchased a bottle of wine, we finally watched him pull his Lexus into the garage of an old brownstone off of 29th Street. It was a nice neighborhood; the streets were lined with tall trees and the lawns were manicured to a perfect green. We parked across the street and flew from the car to the shadowed area within the park that sat slightly to the east of their residence.

After feeding from a couple who'd been strolling in the park, I made sure the street was clear before Loni and I crept towards the house. We took care to remain as stealthy as possible, since we were still unsure of the extent of Meredith's demons powers. There was no need for us to worry though, as we found them very occupied and distracted. From what we were seeing, it looked like Rose's father was enjoying being with the demon *very* much.

We spent the night watching the house from the car. After their lovemaking ended, they went to bed like any normal couple would do. We used our enhanced hearing to listen as Meredith washed her face while Jeremy brushed his teeth, then they slid into bed and slept until their alarm woke them. We were still up at 5 a.m. as the sun had yet to rise. But knowing it would happen soon, we had to decide where we were going to hide for the day, because after we called Evie to report their inactivity, she asked that we stay for another night to see if we could catch a break of any kind.

"What about the hotel we saw just around the block? We wouldn't even have to move the car, we could just run there and check in," Loni suggested. She hated being in the car.

We'd recently returned from our honeymoon in Europe, where we'd trekked across the region during the night, hiding and sleeping in hotel rooms with "Do Not Disturb" signs hung from the doors during the day. It had apparently become our "thing."

"Sure thing, crumpet. That sounds like a good idea. We'll leave the car here so we don't lose our spot. Let me just grab our things out of the boot and we'll knock off." We climbed out of the car and I took note of how soon the sun would be up. It was something that was built-in to our vampire DNA. We had less than two hours before the sun rendered us comatose, so we started walking down the sidewalk towards the hotel. After a few steps, I took one last look back at the brownstone and saw Jeremy looking out their bedroom window from the second story. *Bloody hell.* We were busted.

My gut instinct was to grab Loni, and with our vampire speed, get the hell out of dodge. But I didn't want to give Jeremy any more fodder to fuel his assumptions. So instead, I reached out for Loni's hand and hoped it looked like we were just a young couple out for a stroll. *At five in the morning...yeah right.*

I didn't risk turning around again, and in just a few minutes we reached the hotel, checked in, and hung the Do Not Disturb sign on the door. With the locks in place, Loni headed for the loo to take a bath and I dialed Evie to check in one last time before nodding off.

"I think Jeremy saw us."

"Don't worry. Your recent absence is something that will work in our favor. Neither Jeremy or Meredith have seen you or Loni here before. Get some rest, but as soon as you wake, head back to the car and see if you can find out anything that could be of help to us."

"Roger that, Evie. Goodnight."

"Goodnight, Renard."

CHAPTER TWELVE

Falling Apart

(Christian)

After Rose's and my fight, I left our room once more, slamming the door in my wake. I was so mad at the way Rose was acting. It had been really hard to hear she was feeling like a prisoner here. How could being with the person you love feel like a prison? And I loved her beyond measure. So much so, that I had recently gotten a tattoo to demonstrate the very fact.

It was three words done in Slavic runes: Truly, Madly, Deeply. It was located on my upper right shoulder-blade and was meant to describe how I lived and loved. I loved Rose with all my heart, but I was starting to question if she still felt the same.

I understood finding out Meredith was alive changed the situation for her...for all of us. It had been good news that Rose wasn't a wanted criminal, but I knew, once again, she feared for her father's safety. What I didn't understand was why this had changed things between us.

"Hey. Can I talk to you?"

I hadn't realized I was in front of Terrance's cell until he'd called out.

"What do you want to talk about?" I leaned against the opening of his cell and watched as he paced what little distance he could while still chained to the wall.

"Have you found out where that demon bitch is yet?"

"Evie has Renard and Loni checking it out. They're supposed to be back tomorrow night."

"I'm going to kill her, Christian. Just find out where she is and let me out of here and all our problems will be over. I'll make her pay for what she did to Loraine and me."

I remembered Terrance expressing his feelings for Loraine when Rose and I had questioned him months ago, but none of us had talked about it since.

"Did you really love her?"

"Yes." Exhaling, he stopped his angry pacing and leaned his back against the cell's gray cinderblock wall. "She was honestly the first person I loved since I'd been turned and lost my family." As his shoulders sagged and his head dropped, I realized that I finally felt sorry for him.

"Well, as soon as we learn how to kill her, I'll let you know. But honestly, I'm not sure Evie will let you out even though you're obviously drifting back. She won't risk that Meredith may still have the ability to control you. This may be a fight you're just going to have to sit out."

His chains rattled as he started drifting and pacing again. "She killed Loraine and messed with my mind! Made me lie to everyone I cared about and to Rose. She has to be stopped, and I want revenge for Loraine. I loved her, Christian. I really did."

"Then you and Rose have a common goal."

It was in that moment I realized I wouldn't be biting a human to guard Rose during the day. She needed to meet with her dad and start planning revenge for her mother. She hadn't killed Meredith the first time, but with all of our help...she wouldn't fail again.

"Hang in there, Terrance. I'll let you know what we find out."

CHAPTER THIRTEEN

Merry Little Men

(Meredith)

"I'm impressed." The logging site Damien had scouted really was ideal. Merry little men hustled around doing their manly work, yet in the last designated area of the site there were only two workers, far removed from the rest of the crew. "Let's go check out the hunting shack and get everything set up, and then we'll head back down here just before quitting time."

"Ok, boss. Sounds good. Let me grab the stuff from my truck."

I watched Damien gather his supplies as I did the same. We were parked far enough from the work site, along a lone dirt road, that if anyone happened to stumble upon our vehicles they would most likely think they belonged to a couple of hikers exploring the woods.

"Do you have everything?" I asked.

"Si. Do you need me to carry anything for you?"

"No. Let's just get this over with. I want to have everything set up before sundown, so when the final horn of the day blows we can just grab them and go."

The excitement on his face was clear. He couldn't wait to kill these men and get another taste of fresh blood.

"Do you think if we moved this week's meeting up to tonight all of your cousins would be able to attend?"

"I think so. But why do you want to move it up? So the blood will be fresher?"

"Actually, it's because I saw a strange car outside my house this afternoon before I left. I think the vampires have found me and I need to get our people ready to fight as soon as possible."

"Are you sure it's the vampires?"

"No, but I won't risk it. I'm going to check the car out tonight when I return home, but I think it's better to be safe than sorry. Call your cousins and tell them the meeting's tonight."

"You got it."

* * * * *

(Jeremy)

As the squawk of my morning alarm penetrated my ears, I slowly started to wake. But suddenly, the alarm wasn't the only noise piercing the silence. A car door slammed outside my bedroom window, followed by the chirp of its alarm being set.

This was usually a very quiet neighborhood, and not many people were out the door before me. So, I sluggishly made my way to the window to take a look. The moment I noticed the young couple walking down the sidewalk, my weary eyes popped open and my paranoia revved into high gear. The car they just left parked across the street looked like the one from last night–the one that had been following me.

The young man glanced back at the car and then met my eyes for a split second. He wasn't anyone I recognized, and neither he nor his girlfriend looked menacing, just out of place. They resembled what I'd describe as a couple of European grunge pop stars. At least that's how Rose described some of the bands she used to watch on MTV.

Rose. I missed my girl so much, and now having this couple show up here, a couple that I was sure had followed me from The Rising Pit...I had to get back there and continue my search.

Maybe this weekend I would take Meredith out for a night on the town. A night that would include dancing...at The Rising Pit. When I'd been there looking for Rose it seemed like a really nice club, and hopefully, if I could spend a little time inside, I might just discover the clue I needed to find my daughter.

Dinner, dancing, and some detective work sounded like the perfect weekend to me.

* * * * *

(Damien)

I was so happy Meredith was pleased with my plan. I'd remembered this logging site from when my cousin had been one of their part-time workers a few months back. It was notorious for always having different workers constantly coming and going. Once I'd scouted the area I figured the far back parcel would be the perfect place to snag some blood donors.

I gathered my supplies: some drugs, needles, pipes, etc., and the tubs we were going to be draining the blood into, and then headed over to Meredith.

She was so beautiful. Her long blonde hair and that tight little ass. I'd blamed my reaction in the alley on the blood high I'd been experiencing, but really, it was because I'd wanted her from the moment we met.

I worked on the east side of town as a construction manager, and very rarely had a need to travel into the city, but on that particular day I was headed downtown to drop off some building permits. That's where I'd first laid eyes on Meredith.

She and Jeremy were having lunch at one of the outdoor cafés that littered the downtown area. The moment I laid eyes on her my body reacted. Desire flowed through my veins like hot lava. Not only was she sexy, but the red flare in her eyes had me assuming both she and Jeremy were demons. *Finally, another female demon that wasn't related to me.*

After gaining control, I'd walked past the lovebirds and went about my business, but on my way back out she'd been sitting alone and waved me over.

We started talking and she explained that she realized I was a demon when my eyes flared as I walked by the table earlier. I guess I hadn't hidden my reaction to her as well as I thought I had. She told me that Jeremy was still in the dark about his heritage, but that she was planning to set up a group where demons could get together and discuss their ancestry. She was happy to hear I had a large extended family that I thought would like to attend.

"Do you have everything?" she asked, pulling my attention back to the present.

"Yes. Do you need me to carry anything for you?"

"No. Let's just get this over with. I want to have everything set up before sundown, so when the final horn of the day blows we can just grab them and go."

She was so strong and in control, and that was fucking sexy. I couldn't wait to see how she handled herself tonight. How she would use her demon strength and speed to take care of business.

I wasn't sure if I would be able to control my lust for her a second time.

CHAPTER FOURTEEN

Shocked

(Rose)

I felt the tears soaking my face before I even realized I was crying again. I'd been so shocked when Christian stormed out of our room after our second fight of the day.

What had he meant when he said I was wrong if I thought he couldn't stop me? He better not be thinking of biting me and using his sedative on me or else this whole charade would be over in a heartbeat.

As things stood right now, it wouldn't be too far of a stretch for people to think I'd walked away after finding out Christian had been keeping things from me. That was a "typical" reason people broke up all the time. The problem was...I loved him and I wished I didn't have to leave, not to mention I had nowhere to go.

I couldn't go back to my house and I couldn't go after my dad since Meredith was there waiting for me. I didn't think she was controlling him, even though I couldn't tell Christian and his clan that. They'd wonder how I knew or what made me so sure. The fact that he was a demon would be the first clue, but I wasn't even sure that was an accurate assumption. God, this was such a mess.

A knock at the door startled me. I wiped the tears from my face as I crossed the room.

I opened the door to see Evie's smiling face. "May I come in?"

"Sure."

"Thank you. Do you mind if we sit and talk for a moment?"

"Sure." I sounded like a broken record. I wasn't sure what Evie would have to talk to me about, and I really wasn't in the mood for another speech about how much Christian loved me. I knew he loved me, but unfortunately that didn't matter anymore.

"I wanted to talk to you about Terrance." Evie sat on the edge of the bed and I slowly eased down beside her.

That was a shock. "Okay. What about him?"

"I'd like to talk about the time you spent with him while your mother was alive."

Oh hell no. This was not something I wanted to get into with Evie. When I explained all those months ago that Terrance had been the first vampire I'd met, I told them that while everything he said had been a lie, he'd never hurt my mom. What else could she possibly want to know?

"Specifically, I want to talk about Terrance's relationship with your mother. You said he was always very gentle with her, but do you truly believe that he loved her?"

"Um...I'm not sure. Like I said before, he never hurt her and always treated her like she was special to him, but in love with her? I...I just don't know. Why does it matter? My mom's gone and even if he did love her, she loved my dad...not Terrance."

"I know that, Rose. Please understand, I'm not trying to insinuate they were having an affair, but Terrance has claimed he wants vengeance on Meredith for killing your mom...the woman he loved."

I was suddenly on my feet. "What? He wants to go after Meredith to avenge my mom?"

"Yes, that's what he said."

"Well, isn't that a good thing? That he's remembering and wanting to go after her?"

"Yes, I'm very happy he's showing signs of drifting back and that his memories are returning. But what I'm concerned about is that he may be using his feelings for your mother as an excuse to get released, when instead he could be following Meredith's commands without our knowledge. That's why I'm asking your opinion. Looking back, do you think he was *truly* in love with your mother?"

I thought about my response and knew what I'd say could make a difference in Terrance's release or not. But if he was willing to go after the person who killed my mom, I thought the risk was worth it. "Yes. Thinking back to their interactions, I could definitely see that he was in love with her."

"Alright. Thank you, Rose. I have a lot to think about, but just know that as soon as I hear from Balam I'll call a meeting to discuss our plans to go after Meredith. I want to make sure you'll be there. No more secrets, I promise."

"Thank you, Evie. That means a lot to me."

I watched as she gracefully made her way out the door and thought to myself...*no more secrets? Yeah, right.*

* * * * *

(Christian)

As I rounded the corner at the end of the hall, I saw Evie knocking on Rose's and my door. She rarely entered our private rooms, so I was more than curious about her presence here.

I watched as Rose answered the door and then Evie disappeared inside. I thought now was as good a time as any to practice my newly developing skills, so I eased up to the door and flattened myself against the outside wall.

I'd never tried to use my *super-hearing* on purpose before, so I was unsure of how to even begin. But remembering the advice Evie had once given me, I began to relax and concentrated on exactly what I wanted to do.

I took four deep breaths as I imagined my ears opening up to let the outside thoughts around me filter in and then I heard Evie asking Rose, "...but do you truly believe that he loved her?"

I remained calm and listened as Evie continued to talk to Rose about Terrance and his feelings about her mother. But it didn't take long for me to realize that I couldn't hear anything Rose was thinking in response. The thoughts rapidly drifted away and I was left with nothing but my irritation.

Why did Rose still feel like she had to hide her thoughts around us? I knew that was exactly what she was doing because she'd explained Terrance had once informed her it was necessary. At the time though, she didn't know that only Evie and Dax were capable of scanning, and they could only see the thoughts of what you were immediately thinking. We explained all of this to her, and I thought she trusted us enough to no longer feel it was necessary. *Guess I was wrong.*

I supposed I couldn't blame her for not wanting Evie to know what she was thinking at the moment. I'm sure her head was spinning, having to contemplate another man besides her father being in love with her mom. Under those circumstances, I would probably want to keep those thoughts private too.

I let go of my frustration and waited for Evie to emerge from our room. I wanted to ask her why she thought questioning Rose about this was necessary.

She didn't seem surprised to find me waiting outside. "I heard you approach and was scanning you as you tried to use your new ability. I take it you couldn't hear any of Rose's thoughts either?"

"No. But I'm sure it's just a habit of hers at this point. I was thinking about trying with her again later. I'm hoping if I can get my ability to work around her it might give me a clue as to what she's planning and give me an idea of how to smooth things over between us. "

"Alright. Just let me know if you're successful. And to answer your internal question, I'm debating releasing Terrance against Balam's judgment. I have a theory I want to put to the test, and Rose's thoughts about his feelings for her mother may prove important."

"What's your theory?"

"I'm not ready to discuss it yet, but once I have all the puzzle pieces in place, you'll be one of the first to know. Now why don't you give Rose some time alone and accompany me upstairs. There's something else I'd like to talk to you about."

As much as I wanted to enter our room and apologize to Rose yet again, I didn't think it would help at the moment. So following Evie's suggestion, I left Rose alone and trailed behind her as we made our way back up to her office through her private entrance from the pit.

"Have a seat," Evie said, extending an arm in the direction of the couch along the far wall of her office.

Her formality suddenly had me nervous.

"What's up, Evie? What else did you want to talk about?"

"I'd like to discuss you becoming the next Sire. I know I said I'd like to wait to see what other powers you developed first, but honestly, with the situation we're facing, I'd like to perform the Passing of Powers ritual soon. I want to make you a Sire right away."

My gut tightened and I knew I'd begun to drift at her statement. This was such a huge step. For Evie, for me, and especially for Rose. It meant we wouldn't have to wait any longer for her to become a vampire and my consort. I was immediately overjoyed at the thought.

"There's one more thing," Evie continued. "I know it's traditional for a new Sire to take his consort and relocate, beginning their new life somewhere else, but in this case...I'd like you to remain with our clan."

I'd always assumed it was mandatory that the new Sire leave their old clan, so I was thrilled to receive Evie's offer. Leaving my family had always been the one thing I considered a downfall to becoming the next Sire.

"I'd love for me and Rose to stay here with the clan, but isn't that against the rules?"

"I've thought about it, and while leaving your old clan is *traditional* for a new Sire, I don't think it's ever truly been mandatory. I believe it was just a tradition that'd been passed down from Sire to Sire, clan to clan. Regardless, I think it's time we tested the theory, because the real reason I want to speed up this process, is so that when we finally face the demons, we'll have two Sires here instead of just one. We'll deal with whatever conflicts arise after this situation is resolved. Agreed?"

"Agreed. When do you want to do the ritual?"

"Right now."

CHAPTER FIFTEEN

Private

(Rose)

After Evie left my room, I paced around aimlessly trying to gain control of the chaos in my mind. I couldn't believe Terrance had truly loved my mom. When he'd said it all those months ago, I hadn't really processed it at the time. Being faced with the demon who'd killed my mom had been a pretty big distraction. But now, I wasn't sure if it bothered me or was something I should be thankful for. I suppose the time they spent together was safer and more pleasant for Mom considering he did love her. God, I couldn't think about this right now.

I headed up to the club through Evie's private entrance, since coming up from under the stage while the club was in full swing wasn't allowed for obvious reasons. As the bookcase opened into her office, I saw her and Christian sitting on the couch against the far wall. "Excuse me, I didn't mean to interrupt. I'm just going to go blow off some steam on the dance floor if that's alright?"

"I'll be out to find you shortly," Christian replied stiffly.

I didn't respond but instead just walked out into the fray of happy people, bumping and grinding to the sultry beat that filled the air.

I headed to the bar and plopped down on a stool. Tori and Dominique were working their magic as usual. They made really good tips and had a loyal customer base since they were such great bartenders. I'd gotten to know them quite a bit and they were both down to earth, kind hearted, and really funny. I'd spent more time with Dom though, because every chance she got, Tori would leave the club. Dom had explained it was because she didn't get out of the house much when she was human, so now she just loved being outdoors. Right now...I could relate.

I knew I wouldn't be allowed to go outside, especially at night when it was more likely I could run into trouble, but man...I really needed to get away. Find somewhere private and just think.

A light went off in my head. *Private.* The private rooms upstairs. I knew they were used as feeding rooms for the visiting vampires, but if I could find an empty one maybe I could finally get some time alone. Plus, I really wasn't looking forward to Christian "finding me shortly." I wasn't ready to have to put up my walls again. It was getting so hard not to fall into his arms and cry my eyes out. Especially since he explained everything. But, this was for his own good, and I loved him too much to let anything ever happen to him.

Besides, I knew as the years passed, he'd eventually get over me and find someone else.

As the tears flooded my eyes, I pushed off my stool and made my way through the crowd. Once I'd climbed the stairs to the second floor, I took a moment to look around, making sure that Christian hadn't left Evie's office yet. I didn't see him so I started towards the farthest room at the end of the hall. That's when someone grabbed me.

* * * * *

(Christian)

"Now? You want to make me the new Sire right now?"

"Yes. I think the sooner the better. I've told Dax my plan but no one else knows. I think it will be to our advantage to keep it a secret."

"So even if I become the Sire now, you want me to wait to change Rose?"

"I'm sorry, but yes. I think it would be to our benefit if the demons still think we don't have an active Sire that can create new vampires. Plus, I feel that whatever information Balam provides us with in regards to killing them, it will truly be to our advantage having two Sires instead of one. The element of surprise will be on our side."

I considered Evie's plan. It was a good one. I was just extremely nervous. I hadn't thought this day would be upon me for quite some time, and I wasn't sure I could keep this from Rose. "Alright, but even if I can't change Rose yet, I still want to tell her it's done. I don't want to keep any more secrets from her."

"That's fine. But please make sure she understands the necessity of keeping it secret. I don't even want the rest of the clan to know until

I'm ready. I won't risk one of them becoming infected by accident and having this knowledge to share with our enemies."

"Alright. I'm ready. Should we go downstairs?"

Evie looked at the door and the lock slammed into place. I was always forgetting telekinesis was one of the powers she developed during her triggering. "We'll be undisturbed. Let's begin."

"What do I need to do?" I asked, unsure of my part in all of this.

"Nothing. It's actually a very quick process. I will perform the ritual and say the words, then everything else happens internally. You'll feel a rush of additional strength as the poison of true death and the sedative of eternal life flow into you. Let's begin."

I shifted slightly in my seat and my palms started to sweat. "What if I'm not really the one being triggered? What if this clairaudient power is just something else completely?" I couldn't help but share my insecurities. I was afraid of not being the one, and I didn't want Evie to attempt the ritual if it wasn't meant to be.

"Christian, your clairaudience is just another psychic power which allows you to hear the unspoken. There is no doubt that you're the one. Now please, trust me."

"Okay, Evie. I do."

She instructed me to lie down on the couch as she stood over me with her hands extended. She explained that she would be reading my energy and only when it was time to "pass the powers" would she be biting me. I closed my eyes and listened as she began.

Her voice carried the Sire command as she chanted, "I call on my ancestors, join me now. Flow through me as Christian completes this vow.

The new Sire, he is triggered to be. Now let my powers flow from me."

In the next instant she'd shoved my head to the side and sunk her fangs into my neck. My body arched off the couch as warm liquid flowed into my veins. It felt similar to being turned, but a hundred times more intense.

I was bombarded by a variety of colors layering my mind. I saw sparkling yellow as the sedative of eternal life spread throughout my body. Then flashes of green blinded me as the poison of true death settled deep within my heart. It literally felt as if these powers were filling up special compartments within me, and the strength they carried with them was truly a blessing from the gods. The last thing to happen was the scanning ability snapping into place.

As soon as Evie released me, I bolted off the couch and grabbed my head. The noise was too much for me to bear. I assumed this was an

unforeseen side-effect of the scanning ability

combining with my clairaudience. But whatever it

was, it sucked.

I was suddenly overwhelmed with the loud

noises of everything and everyone in the vicinity.

The club's music, people calling out their orders to

Dom and Tori. Pieces of conversation rang

through my head like a cacophony of squawking

birds, and then I heard the one thing that

overshadowed all the rest...Rose's scream.

CHAPTER SIXTEEN

In Trouble

(Renard)

After spending the day comatose in the hotel, Loni and I awoke with the sun's disappearance, and immediately started making our plans for the night.

"Do you think Jeremy knows who we are? Are we in trouble here?" Loni asked.

"No, poppet, we don't need to worry. Jeremy isn't a threat. Even if he was daft enough to attack us, we could easily rectify the situation by biting him and making him forget. No, I'm not worried about him. But we do have to worry about Meredith. We need to see what she's up to, so my suggestion for tonight is to again, feed in the park, but then we need to move the car and keep watch from a different location. Hopefully she'll make a move that will shed some light on her powers or possibly her intentions."

"Alright, my love. Sounds like a plan." Loni kissed me, long and deep, and if we didn't need to rush to move our car from its present location, I would have sank back down onto the bed and relived some of the other fond memories from our honeymoon.

* * * * *

(Meredith)

Snagging the two workers had gone just as planned. As the horn signaled the end of the their day, we used our strength and speed to knock them out and rush them to the abandoned hunting shack.

I could tell Damien was having a hard time keeping his desire to drink from these humans in check. But after I told him he could have a small sip to begin the draining process, his mood quickly improved.

"I can't believe how quickly the changes take effect. I can feel my strength increase almost immediately." He made his point by slamming his fist through the solid log wall.

"What the hell are you doing?" I dropped the human I was holding and flew to within an inch of his face. "We've taken care to set this whole scene, and you think slamming a hole through the wall isn't going to raise a few questions?"

"Who cares? If anyone did track this scene back to us, I'd kill them. Problem solved."

"Problem solved? Problem solved?" My rage was boiling over, and I was sure my eyes were glowing red. I slammed him against the wall he'd just put the hole in. He may have just gained a boost in strength, but there was no way he could compare to me. "You listen to me, you blood-hungry asshole. I will not let you put everything I'm working towards in jeopardy by leaving a trail of bodies across this city. What we're doing has to be kept on the down low. I can't risk the vampire's finding out."

He pushed off the wall, shrugging out of my grasp. I let him go. "Fine. I'm sorry. I won't kill anyone without your *permission*." He paced the room, looking at the bodies on the floor. After a sigh, he continued, sounding remorseful. "I'll fix the hole. I have a sledgehammer in my truck we could leave here as evidence. I'll wipe it down so all we'll have to do is put one of these guys' prints on it and we should be in the clear. A sledgehammer could easily put a hole like that through a wall this old."

For being as hot-headed as he was just moments ago, his plan actually had merit. I was pretty sure it would work. "Okay. Hurry and go get the hammer. I'll finish draining these two and make sure all the animal scratches and drugs are in place."

"Okay. And Meredith, I really am sorry."

I gave him a quick nod and watched as he sped out the door. It was becoming apparent I would have to monitor his blood intake. This whole situation was an unknown for both of us, but it was obvious that drinking human blood affected different people in different ways.

I became euphoric after drinking Loraine's blood, but I hadn't gone insane or power hungry. Yes, I would definitely be keeping an eye on Damien. I couldn't risk having a loose cannon as my second in command. And if he ever felt like pushing my boundaries, he'd find out that only a stronger demon could kill another demon, and I'd be making sure that I remained the strongest demon of them all.

With this exact plan in mind, I pulled out the extra bag I'd brought and began siphoning off some extra blood for my personal stores, of course taking a moment to have a small taste. The warm blood flowing down my throat filled me again with strength and joy. I could feel I was truly becoming immortal. Those vampires would have to be pretty fucking stupid if they thought they stood a chance against me.

Damien returned just as I'd finished draining the second body. He swallowed hard as he saw the last drop of blood hit the container. I began our cleanup and removed all the IV equipment from our victims and then staged their bodies like we'd planned, adding the sledgehammer as the final touch.

"It looks good. Really believable," Damien said.

"Yes it does. The claw marks, blood, and fur certainly give it that wild feel we need." I laughed as we carried out the containers of blood and the rest of our supplies. "Did you get a hold of your family? Are they going to be able to make tonight's meeting?"

"Yes. They will all be there, though only a few are aware of what's happening. I told you I knew certain members of my family would be down with drinking blood, but I've instructed them not to say anything to the others. We should be able to spike the drinks as planned and everyone will begin gaining strength and speed by the end of the night."

"Thank you, Damien. I appreciate your help. Now we just have to keep that temper of yours in check. No more blood for you tonight, okay?"

"I agree. I think I've reached my limit for today."

Watching his jaw twitch had me questioning his statement. I wasn't convinced I wouldn't have a problem with him at tonight's meeting. Maybe, I'd better start looking for someone else to help me in my efforts. I'd have to pay special attention to everyone's reaction to the blood tonight. Maybe one of his relatives would display a little more self-control.

Once we reached our vehicles and stowed our bounty, I explained the plan for tonight's meeting. "I'm going to run home and change then I'll meet you at the conference hall. I want to get there around 7:45 p.m., so we'll be able to set up and spike the drinks in advance."

"Sounds good. I have to run home too, and then I'll meet you there. Should I bring a bottle of champagne so we can toast the beginning of your army?"

I knew he was teasing, but it didn't sound like a bad idea. After tonight, the vampires wouldn't stand a chance.

CHAPTER SEVENTEEN

Biting

(Rose)

The moment I was grabbed, I started screaming. I tried digging my heels into the floor as I was being drug into one of the private rooms, but suddenly a set of fangs pierced the side of my neck.

Oh shit! This could not be happening. Who in the world would risk Christian's anger by biting me? It had to be a vampire from outside of town. Someone who didn't know who I was.

He must have used his sedative to quiet my screams because in the next second I was completely calm...on the outside. But once my thoughts cleared, allowing me to focus on the nightmare this was going to become, my internal panic really set in.

I tried to pull away, but the vampire's fangs sunk deeper as he held me tight from behind. *Fuck!* I couldn't believe this was happening. I assumed that in only a few minutes my demon blood would start infecting whoever this vampire was. How the hell was I supposed to explain why this vampire drifted dark after biting me? My situation just went from bad to worse.

I didn't have any idea if it would work, but I knew I'd better try something fast. I wasn't even sure *how* to do it, but I focused on my anger and tried to release my demon side. Maybe I could forge a mind bond and force this asshole to stop.

Thankfully, I must have done something right, because all of a sudden I felt the connection of the mind bond and I could almost see what was happening through *his* eyes. I projected the thoughts that I wanted him to feel, adding a verbal command for good measure. *Stop NOW!*

The vampire went rigid behind me and his fangs withdrew immediately. Luckily, I could feel and see through our connection that he used his sedative to heal the wounds in my neck. The instant his fangs slid free, the puncture marks closed and it looked as if they never even existed.

I immediately spun around and shoved the vampire with all my strength. He let out a little *humph* as he landed on the red velvet couch. I didn't recognize him, but that didn't mean much since the only other vampire in the area I knew besides Christian's clan, was Justin. He was a handsome guy with a decent build, and he wore a black leather jacket. His hair was short and blonde, but I knew that would start to change any moment.

"Who are you? What's your name?" I nudged his mind so he didn't have any choice but to respond.

"My name is Kennedy."

"Where are you from?"

"Florida."

"What are you doing here, and how did you find out about The Rising Pit?" I had to speed this up, because like I assumed, his hair and eyes had already begun to drift dark.

"I was on vacation and visiting some friends outside of Masen. They told me about the club, and I thought I'd check it out before heading back home."

The guilt was building inside of me. Just because this vampire had made the mistake of biting *me*, he was going to lose all sense of right and wrong and possibly end up facing the true death. It sucked, but I had to face the hard reality...I couldn't allow him to leave. Letting him go knowing he'd drift darker and darker and start hurting innocent people was just not an option.

"Okay, Kennedy. You're going to sit here and not move until someone comes to find you. Do you understand?"

"Sit here and not move. Yes, I understand."

"And you aren't going to remember anything about biting me or what I looked like either. Got it?"

"Yes. I don't remember you."

Wow. This mind bond thing could prove really useful. I just wished I had more time to test out my demon powers. But unfortunately right now was not that time. I had to get as far away from this scene as possible, and fast.

I parted the velvet curtains a fraction of an inch and peeked outside to make sure no one was coming. The coast was clear so I rushed from the room and ran down the stairs into the bathroom. The moment I was inside, I nudged the door open a crack so I could see what was happening.

It didn't take long before I saw Christian, Evie, and Dax heading towards the stairs. The moment they hit the top I shot across the dance floor and into Evie's office. I found the button on the bookshelf that opened the secret door to her private entrance into the pit, and made my way back to my room in a hurry.

I thought the best thing for me to do was pretend that once I finished dancing, I used the restroom and then headed back down here to get some rest. I just hoped that no one saw me upstairs, or I could kiss that story goodbye.

* * * * *

(Christian)

After having Rose's scream penetrate the chaos inside my mind, I was able to focus and gain my bearings.

"Christian, what's wrong?" The panicked look on Evie's face confirmed that this wasn't a normal reaction to the Passing of Powers ritual.

"My head is splitting and I can hear everything...including Rose's scream. She's in trouble."

I shoved off the couch and flew towards the door. As much as I wanted to use my now enhanced vampire speed to dash straight upstairs, I knew I couldn't. Not with all the human patrons filling the club tonight.

As Evie and I wove our way through the crowd, I noticed her motion for Dax to join us. The three of us quickly made our way to the stairs which led to the second floor and the private rooms. I knew this was where Rose's scream originated from. I wondered if becoming a Sire heightened all my abilities including my claircognizance, but right now, all the questions I had would have to wait. I had to find Rose.

After reaching the private room that held her scent, I threw open the velvet curtains to find a young male vampire sitting on the couch alone.

"Who are you and what are you doing here?" Evie demanded.

"My name is Kennedy, and I'm just sitting here. Is that a crime?"

Dax took a step forward, his hair starting to slightly drift from blonde to light brown. Talking like that to a Sire, let alone his consort, was a really bad idea.

Suddenly Kennedy launched himself at Dax and the two of them went crashing into the table, followed by the chairs and walls.

"Enough!" Evie's voice still held her Sire's command, and even though Kennedy wasn't a part of our clan, vampires had no choice but to obey a Sire when in their presence.

The two froze, hands still wrapped around each other's necks. I decided this was a good time to test my Sire's voice as well, since Dax already knew we'd completed the ritual, and I could easily force this outsider to keep his mouth shut. "Kennedy, sit down and don't move." *Excellent.* It worked.

The vampire eyed me as he slowly moved back towards the couch. That was when I noticed his eyes and hair were both drifting darker by the minute. *Oh no!*

"Evie, we got a problem."

"What is it, Christian? What are you sensing?"

"Nothing. That's the problem. I can hear tiny whispers but they're becoming distorted and fuzzy. And look at him...he's starting to drift dark. I think we have a demon in the club."

CHAPTER EIGHTEEN

Speeding

(Renard)

Once Loni and I had moved our car to a new spot around the corner, we took a few moments to feed in the park before checking to see if anyone was home at Jeremy and Meredith's.

After verifying no one was there, we launched ourselves into the nearest tree to secure a good position from which to spy. It was a bloody good thing it was mid-summer and the trees were in full bloom, because if it'd been winter and the trees were sparse, I didn't think Loni and I would've made very convincing monkeys.

"This is perfect. I can see right into their living room and bedroom windows. Now all we have to do is wait," Loni said.

I glanced at my watch and assumed we wouldn't have to wait too long before someone made an appearance. It was 7:02 p.m., and even if Jeremy had made another trip to Masen for the day, he should be returning home at any moment. However, to my surprise and satisfaction, it was Meredith who arrived home first.

Loni and I watched as she parked on the street instead of pulling into the garage. Her rushed pace and the fact that she left her car running was a clear indication she was still on the move. Good news for us.

We remained hidden in the tree as Meredith burst from her home in a flash of speed that rivaled any vampire's. She'd changed clothes and was obviously in a big hurry to get somewhere, which was going to be a problem since our car was currently parked around the corner.

"Looks like we'll be following on foot," I said.

"Fantastic!" The giddiness in Loni's voice reminded me how much she loved running free through the night. Maybe this wouldn't be such a boring assignment after all.

* * * * *

(Jeremy)

As I drove home I thought about my plan for the weekend and was excited to fill Meredith in. But just as I rounded the corner at the end of the block, I saw Meredith speeding away from our townhome. Suddenly there was a blur of motion in the park across the street but my ringing cell phone quickly diverted my attention.

"Hi, honey. I'm just pulling into the drive. Where are you speeding off to?"

"My meeting this week has been pushed up to tonight. I shouldn't be too late though. How was your day?"

"It was pretty good. Nothing too exciting, but I do have some exciting plans for this weekend I want to share with you."

"Oooohhh...exciting plans, I like the sound of that. What are they?"

"I was hoping we could go out for dinner and dancing...at The Rising Pit."

Silence filled the line so I looked at my phone as I exited the car. Maybe I'd hit the mute button by mistake. "Mer? Did you hear me?"

"Yes. I heard you. But Jeremy, I think this is something we need to talk about first."

Well, this was unexpected. I thought she'd be more than excited to have an evening out, especially since she'd been so busy with work and this new group she'd been chairing lately. And honestly, I wasn't sure what there was to talk about. She knew I'd wanted to go back to the club since I'd struck out the first time, not to mention my failure again last night.

As I made my way inside, I could feel my frustration levels start to rise...literally. I was starting to sweat as I felt a flush of heat spread across my face. "Alright. I guess we'll talk about it when you get home."

I didn't wait for a response. I just closed my phone and threw it onto the counter along with my keys. For some reason, this was really pissing me off. I couldn't understand why she'd want to stop me from looking for Rose. Not after she'd been the one to protect her in the first place.

By the time I pounded up the stairs, I was fuming mad, which was not a good thing. I couldn't afford to lose my temper again, because lately...something strange happened when I did.

* * * * *

(Damien)

After I changed my clothes, I headed over to the warehouse where I'd stashed the body of the woman I'd hid earlier in the day. I knew Meredith wouldn't approve, but I couldn't help it. The taste of human blood was now my new drug of choice. I'd had my fair share of others in the past, but none surpassed the high that fresh blood gave me.

The feeling of strength and power that flowed into me every time I tasted the sweetness of human blood was enough to have me salivating before I even entered the warehouse.

I made my way to the back of the abandoned building and found my donor in the same spot as I'd left her. She was pale, most likely from the blood loss I'd inflicted earlier, but other than that—

and the puncture wounds that were visible on her neck—she looked perfectly fine.

She was sitting on the concrete floor with her knees drawn up and was leaning against the metal wall for support. Her long, baggy dress was draped over her knees and hung loose to the ground. It was the same mousy brown color as her hair. I could tell she was either sleeping or passed out, so I approached quietly. As I lifted her slack head, she began to wake.

I'd taken care to gag her earlier so I wouldn't have to hear her high pitched screams again. Once she finally came to and realized her situation hadn't changed, the fear that radiated from her made my skin tingle. Tears filled her eyes and she continually shook her head back and forth as whimpering sounds escaped from beneath the rag in her mouth.

I knew I wouldn't be able to show restraint this time, since only a small amount of blood had almost sent me into a frenzy only a short while ago. Unable to wait any longer I sunk my teeth into the same spots I'd created before.

The sweet taste of ecstasy flowed down my throat and filled my body with an enormous dose of strength.

I didn't care what Meredith said; I wouldn't be limiting my blood intake anytime soon. Besides, it would only prove to benefit her in the end. When we finally faced these vampires, I'd be just as strong as her, and together we would decimate them.

CHAPTER NINETEEN

New Prisoner

(Christian)

Dax didn't have any problems taking our new prisoner through the club since I'd used my Sire command to instruct Kennedy to follow without causing trouble. Once we reached the office, Evie and I remained behind as Dax took Kennedy below in order to get him chained up.

"How the hell are we suppose to tell who's a demon and who's not?" I asked.

"I don't know, Christian. Our scanning ability won't work on a demon because of their built in mental blocks. And I won't risk ending up unconscious like before."

I paced the office, trying to come up with a plan that would weed out the demon in our midst. Unfortunately, I was drawing a blank. We couldn't scan it, we couldn't bite it, and if the demon was anything like Meredith, it would be almost as strong and as fast as we were. This was quickly shaping up to be a lose-lose situation.

I watched as Evie lowered herself onto the couch. I could tell she was upset from her drifting appearance, and it was obvious she was deep in thought. Suddenly, her head snapped up. "I wonder if the fact that we originated from Camazotz, and demons originated from his father Yum Camil, somehow puts them higher up in the hierarchy of things."

Evie had a point. It would make sense that the race created by the demon god, the *father* of our creator, would be stronger and have more powers and built-in defenses, leaving vampires second best. *Fuck me.*

I was just about to sink into the couch and embrace the hopelessness I was starting to feel, when suddenly, once again thanks to my claircognizance, I simply *knew* what we needed to do. "Alright. Let's close down the club and get everyone out of here. Hopefully, by dispersing the crowd we can prevent anyone else from biting the demon tonight...whoever it is. Then we just have to wait until the demons blood leaves Kennedy's system and he should start to drift back like Terrance did. Once that happens, we'll be able to find out who the demon was that he bit."

"That sounds like a reasonable plan, and hopefully we'll hear back from Balam tomorrow and finally gain some insight on exactly how to combat these beasts."

Evie stood and hugged me tightly. "See, Christian. You're going to make a wonderful Sire."

I watched her walk out of the office to start the evacuation of the club. It made me happy to know she had such confidence in me, but at the moment, I didn't feel like a wonderful Sire. I felt like a complete loser. I was so distraught over how all of this would affect my clan that I'd almost forgotten what had started this whole situation...Rose's scream.

I raced towards the bookcase and hit the button to open the secret door to the pit. I was overwhelmed with concern about Rose's involvement in this. I feared that if someone hurt her, I would end up killing every single person in this club, regardless of whether or not I was infected by the demon's blood. If they'd hurt Rose, drifting dark was a price I was willing to pay if it meant putting an end to the demon.

(Rose)

I heard footsteps and voices in the hall, followed by the rattling of chains. I didn't have to look to know that they were chaining up Kennedy at the opposite end of Terrance's cell. There was only one holding cell in the pit, but it was big enough to house three prisoners at once. *Two down, one to go.*

Though if Terrance continued to drift back, the prisoner count would soon be back to one. *Oh, crap!*

If Terrance was drifting back because Meredith's blood had left his system then that meant unless I found a way to slip Kennedy my blood on a continual basis, he'd start drifting back too.

Looks like I'd be finding a way to leave here sooner than later. But not before talking to Christian, apparently, because in a blur of speed he flew into our room and suddenly I found myself nestled tightly against him.

"Oh my god, Rose. I'm so glad you're okay." He continued to hold me close as the rise and fall of his chest slowly returned to a steady pace.

I slowly pulled out of his hug and eased myself down onto the bed. "Christian, what's wrong? Why wouldn't I be okay?"

The puzzled look on his face had me sweating bullets. I didn't know if sticking to my story was a good idea at this point or not. I decided to see what he said next before incriminating myself with a lie that could possibly blow up in my face.

"I heard you scream. And I just left a private room where we located a vampire that we think drank from a demon. The room was covered with your scent."

Dammit! Time to put my acting skills to the test. "You're kidding me! A demon? Here?" I've never detested myself more than I did right now.

"Yes. We think so, but since there's no sure way to tell, we had to chain the vampire up and we'll be waiting until he drifts back to get the exact identity of the demon he bit."

I didn't know what to say or do. I felt the walls closing in on me, and all I wanted to do was run. But run where? I still had nowhere to go that wouldn't lead back to my dad and Meredith. If I went to Jillian's, her parents would notify my dad for sure. Actually, if I showed up on any of my old friends' doorsteps, I was sure my dad and Meredith would be on the scene within hours. I thought of going to stay with Justin's clan, but there was no way that would work either. They would notify Evie and Christian, and that certainly wouldn't end well.

Maybe I should just leave the state completely. Start over somewhere new. Somewhere where I didn't know the local vampires or demons, and live my life like a normal human girl again.

"Rose. Why were you in that room? And what are you thinking about?" Christian's voice was layered with suspicion and I thought I'd been busted without even saying a word.

"Everything. Nothing. I guess I'm just in shock thinking about all of this." My vague answer must have been enough to trigger his protective side, because he sat down on the bed next to me and gathered me in his arms once again, thankfully ignoring the fact that I hadn't answered the first part of his question.

"I know things have been tense between us, but Rose, you have to know I would never let anything happen to you. I love you so much and I'll do anything to protect you."

Tears filled my eyes and I couldn't help but sink into his embrace. I'd missed this so much. Being held by the man I loved, and feeling how perfectly we fit together. Knowing he was strong and that I had nothing to fear as long as I was with him. Yes...this was every girl's dream. Too bad it was currently my nightmare. Before I had a chance to pull away and put the necessary distance between us once again, his next statement left me reeling.

"I have something important I need to tell you. Only Evie, Dax and I know, but once I tell you, you have to keep it a secret. Not even the others can know about it." He took a deep breath and placed both hands on my shoulders, pulling away only enough to look me in the eyes. "Evie and I completed the Passing of Powers ritual earlier tonight...I'm now officially the new Sire."

CHAPTER TWENTY

Meeting

(Meredith)

I didn't know how I was going to get out of
accompanying Jeremy to that damn club. It was
obvious by the snap of his phone, that I'd pissed
him off when I'd said we should talk about it first.
Oh well. I wasn't willing to risk my life by walking
into the enemy's lair just so he could go searching
for that half-breed daughter of his.

I took a few deep breaths, cleared my mind,
and prepared myself for tonight's meeting.
Everything else, including Jeremy's "exciting plans"
were just going to have to be dealt with later.

It was 7:40 p.m. and apparently I'd arrived
before Damien. I hurried to gather the containers
of blood and the rest of the supplies for tonight's

festivities while trying to contain my annoyance that he wasn't already here to help.

The conference hall was a large facility on the bottom floor of an office building that had been closed down last year. The owners kept the bottom level open and used it to book meetings, conferences, wedding receptions or whatever else would pay the bills while they negotiated with investors as to what to do with the place. It worked perfectly for me, because there was never any worry of random people showing up uninvited to our meetings.

I set up the tables, taking extra care to cover them with the nice tablecloths I'd brought along. I wanted to make sure that our food and *drink* station was extra appealing tonight. After setting up the four large crystal bowls and the cups and utensils along the long table, I finally began mixing the punch. I couldn't help but giggle. This punch was definitely going to pack a "punch."

Just as I finished putting the last dose of blood into the mixes, I heard Damien's truck pull up outside. Glancing at my watch, I breathed a sigh of relief because even though he was running slightly late, he'd still arrived just before 8:00 p.m., which gave us a half an hour to go over the plan once more.

He seemed a little disheveled as he came running through the door. Breathing hard he said, "Sorry, boss. I got held up." He finished tucking in his shirt and straightening his tie, and it made me wonder if by "held up" he meant "having sex." Not that I cared.

"No problem. We still have plenty of time to go over things one more time before everyone starts to arrive. But first, take these containers and put them back in the trunk of my car."

I checked my reflection in the mirror hanging on one of the walls while I waited for him to return. My hair was shiny and smooth, and my eyes sparkled with the life essence that flowed through my veins. Anyone looking at me who didn't know the true cause of my glowing, might mistakenly think I was pregnant. *Oh my god!* Could I be pregnant? I hadn't even considered the possibility until just this moment.

"Okay. We're all good. Let's go over the plan once more." Damien's eyes roamed my profile, lingering on the shape of my ass a little too long. That served as the perfect motivator to snap my attention back to the situation at hand. I'd have to ponder motherhood another time.

"Alright. We're going to treat this just like any other meeting. We'll start by welcoming everyone, making sure to introduce anyone who is new. Then I'll talk about our heritage for a bit and what a blessing it is to finally have a demon community that can actually come together...etc., etc. Then we'll invite them to enjoy the food and drink while they mingle."

"Sounds simple enough."

"It may sound simple, but that's when things could get difficult. Once they start to ingest the blood, it *shouldn't* affect them in a noticeable way since it's just a small amount, but obviously since every demon reacts differently to it, we truly have no way of knowing what their reactions will be. What I need you to do is help me monitor everyone in case somebody starts to show signs of the blood's effects."

"No problem. Since most of them are my family any way, it should be easy enough to tell if someone's acting unusual. But for the few who actually know what's going on, can I have them gather in the other room so we can talk to them, and see if they feel anything different?"

"That's a great idea. As everyone arrives, just let those few know that once they start drinking the punch to nonchalantly head towards the first alcove on the right. We can meet them there and question them like you suggested."

I glanced at my watch and felt a rush of energy run through me. It was almost time for people to start arriving. Damien grabbed two glasses and scooped up some of the blood mixture. "Cheers. To the army."

I lifted my glass to his as the smile spread across my face. "To the army."

$$* * * * *$$

(Renard)

We followed Meredith's car by using our vampire speed to hop from shadow to shadow. It took around thirty-five to forty minutes before she parked outside an empty building and headed towards the ground floor.

We stayed hidden for another couple of minutes before moving into the shadows that hugged the east corner of the building. From there we were able to see through one of the small windows into what looked like a large meeting facility.

Meredith was busying herself with setting up tables and a small food spread. But what really drew our interest were the two large containers of blood we saw her haul inside that were now being split between four large punch bowls. Loni and I had smelled the blood the moment she pulled the containers from the boot of her car.

We watched in silence for only a few minutes before an old blue Ford pickup pulled up and parked next to Meredith's car. Our hiding place was apparently perfect because the Hispanic man walking into the building showed no indication of noticing our presence.

As soon as he entered the building, Loni and I focused our vampire hearing, and could now hear their entire conversation. It started off pretty normal until Meredith got to the part about how she was going to talk about their demon heritage and how grateful she was that they now had a community of demons who could get together to discuss their history. *Bloody hell.* Evie was not going to be happy to hear this.

We continued to listen only to be stunned further. Apparently it was Meredith's plan to trick these other demons into ingesting human blood in order to increase their demon powers, and based on what we'd just heard, she was doing this in order to create a demon army.

"This situation just went from a seven to a ten-plus on the 'we're fucked' scale," Loni whispered. I don't think I'd ever seen her this upset. Her hair and eyes had drifted completely black.

"You've got that right, love. We need to get back to The Rising Pit and report this to Evie right away."

We took off at lightning speed to retrieve our car from its present location. The information we now possessed needed to be reported as soon as possible, but I couldn't risk leaving the car behind since the plates were registered to Dax and The Rising Pit.

Once we were safely inside the car and headed back towards Masen, I pulled out my cell and dialed Evie.

"Hello?"

"Evie. We're headed back now and you aren't going to believe what we found out."

Her heavy sigh was the only indication that she wasn't looking forward to our news. And who could blame her? This truly had the potential to send the vampire community into a panic. Demon armies...bugger me.

"Alright. When you arrive, come straight to my office and fill me in. I should be done dealing with our current crisis by then. Once I have all the information, I'll gather everyone together and deliver the news without having to repeat myself. Be safe and we'll see you two soon."

She didn't even give me the chance to ask what the "current crisis" was before hanging up the phone.

"Well, that didn't sound good." Loni's deadpan tone mimicked the sinking feeling in my gut. I looked over at my beautiful wife and her gorgeous hazel eyes, and suddenly wished we'd never returned from England.

CHAPTER TWENTY-ONE

Anger Issues

(Jeremy)

After my infuriating conversation with Meredith, I decided to take a shower in order to *literally* cool off. That was just one of the odd things that had started happening every time I'd gotten angry lately; my body temperature would rise and I'd start sweating like crazy. It was like a volcano was building inside of me, just waiting to explode. The other strange thing...my eyes seemed to get red flecks in them whenever I was about to blow my top.

These reactions, however, weren't the only thing that was confusing me. It was the fact that I'd been getting angry so easily and so much more often than usual. I didn't understand where these anger issues were coming from because I'd never really been an angry kind of guy.

But looking back, that probably had more to do with Loraine than myself. She always was the cheerful, bubbly, and calming one in our relationship, which in turn kept me blissfully happy. I wasn't sure why my relationship with Meredith didn't bring me the same joy, but I suppose it boiled down to the fact that Loraine had truly been my soul mate. *God, I miss her.*

As I turned on the shower and let the steam build, I tried to relax enough to think about what I was going to say to Meredith. Thankfully, I was already starting to feel calmer. It was an amazing thing that always happened whenever I thought of Loraine.

I smiled and shook my head as I stepped into the shower and let the hot water pour over me, washing my irritation down the drain.

(Loraine)

I hovered in my ghostly form above Jeremy as he entered the shower. I longed to be able touch him once again. I tried, but as usual, I watched as my hand misted through his shoulder.

The first time I'd materialized in this spirit form had been a little disorienting. I'd opened my eyes and found myself white and wispy, just like you'd imagine a ghost, staring down at Rose as she cried, curled up on her and Christian's bed deep beneath The Rising Pit.

It felt as if I was a million tiny sparks of energy being fused back together to once again form my body. In the next moment, my mind was flooded with memories. Memories of my life, my death...everything.

I suddenly knew things, like the fact that Christian was a vampire, and that my husband and daughter both had demon blood running through their veins. I knew *everything*. I guessed it was the gods' way of getting me up to speed.

I'd rushed to my Rose and tried to wrap my arms around her, but as I floated down to her and reached out, my hands only misted through her body. I momentarily felt a sense of grief for not being able to hold my daughter, but I was still happy for this chance to even be with her again.

So I watched as Rose's tear-filled shudders calmed and she finally fell asleep, and in that instant I knew the reason for my presence here.

When I was alive I discovered at a very young age that my mere presence had the ability to calm those around me. I'd always considered it a psychic "gift" of some sort. I couldn't manipulate people's emotions, but all I had to do was enter a room and they would physically and mentally relax. And that was why I was here now. To be the calming element in my daughter's life once more. Because since I'd been gone her demon side had started to rise to the surface, and so had Jeremy's.

From that point on I began getting pulled back into my ghost form whenever Rose or Jeremy were either extremely mad, or when they were specifically thinking of me. But the time in between my visits was still a mystery to me. Once I'd disintegrate or disappear there was just nothing...nothing until the next time I formed. No memories of the time in between, but full awareness of everything that had transpired while I was gone.

Now, as I looked down at Jeremy while he relaxed in the shower, I knew that he'd been upset about Meredith's reaction to his plan to visit The Rising Pit. A plan that would help him track down our daughter, providing a little peace for them both. I wish I could figure out how to actually help, or affect things from my ghostly state, but so far I hadn't. I could only hover, watch, and let my calming energy do its job for the people I loved.

CHAPTER TWENTY-TWO

Panic at the Disco

(Rose)

I sucked in a breath as my heart started to
pound out of my chest. I was stunned into silence
as I tried to process Christian's big announcement.
Talk about panic at the disco. I knew exactly what
this meant. He was going to want to change
me...soon. I almost expected him to launch across
the bed and sink his teeth into my neck and turn
me on the spot. I couldn't believe he was officially
the new Sire. And I couldn't believe they
completed the ritual without telling anyone else.

"I don't know what to say. How's this even
possible? You weren't even sure it was really you
who was being triggered." I was trying to stay calm
and get as much information as I could, but I
couldn't deny I was fighting the urge to run

screaming for the door. I didn't know how much longer I was going to be able to deal with all of this.

"I shared my concerns with Evie, but she assured me there was no doubt that it was me. She decided to perform the ritual right away and keep things a secret, so when the time comes to face the demons, the element of surprise, and the fact they'll be facing two Sires instead of just one, will be to our advantage."

I could definitely see her point. It would be an awesome *surprise* for the demons to face, but I was still panicking at the fact that my timeframe for leaving Christian had just been bumped up...again.

"Aren't you happy for me, Rose? For us? Once this nightmare is over, I'll be able to turn you and we can complete the consort ceremony."

I visibly relaxed when I heard the words "*once this nightmare is over.*" Maybe I had more time to plan than I thought.

"Evie doesn't want me to change you right away, as that would pretty much give away our surprise."

Oh, thank god. "I can understand that. And of course I'm happy for you...for us." I stood up and wrapped my arms around him, but made it a point not to linger too long. But as I started to pull away, he grabbed my hips, holding me in place.

"If it was up to me, I'd change you tonight. I can't wait for you to become my consort. The idea of spending eternity with you makes me happier than I can say."

He crushed his lips to mine and our tongues danced their familiar dance. I thought about how all of this—all of my hopes and dreams—would soon be coming to an end, and I couldn't force myself to pull away. Instead, I resigned to selfishly allow myself one last time with the man I loved.

The feel of his lips on mine and the sensation his roaming hands created on my skin had me tingling in all the right places and my stomach fluttering like it was our first time. He ran his hands up my back then weaved them through my hair as I worked the buttons on his shirt.

Shoving the piece of clothing off his shoulders and onto the ground, I broke our kiss, and moved my lips to his neck. The flutter of his pulse under my tongue announced how much he enjoyed when I licked and sucked him there. I lingered briefly until his hands moved to grab my breasts. Squeezing them slightly, he had me arching into his touch.

He groaned as I kissed my way down his chest, moving my hands to his belt. I sat back down on the bed, putting me in the perfect position. Once his belt was loose, I begun to unzip his pants. I raised my eyes to find him drifting rapidly and looking at me with intense desire. Then he tossed his head back in anticipation of the act to come.

That's when we heard a knock on the door.

"Dammit! What is it?" Christian cussed.

"I'm sorry to bother you, but Evie's asked that we all join her upstairs right away," Tori hesitantly announced.

The look on Christian's face was enough to scare anyone, but I knew he was only angry because he was just as desperate to be with me as I was to be with him.

I reached out and ran my hand down his arm. "It's okay. Let's go find out what's going on and we can continue this later." I grabbed his shirt from the floor as he zipped up his pants and fastened his belt.

"All I know is that this better be *seriously* important, or I'm going to have Evie's ass."

Turned out...it was.

We made our way upstairs and all gathered around the now empty club, waiting for Evie to begin.

"Sorry for interrupting everyone's evening, but Renard and Loni have just returned with news."

Apparently they'd driven like a bat out of hell and made it home in just under an hour and a half. I was suddenly very happy Tori had interrupted us, because there was no way I was going to miss what Renard and Loni had to say.

"I gathered all of us here so that I wouldn't have to repeat myself. Our problem with the demons just got much more serious than we ever could've anticipated. Meredith is secretly creating an army of blood drinking demons. An army that will soon be as strong and fast as she is."

The gasps and four letter words that flew around the room, combined with the kaleidoscope of drifting hair colors was almost a funny sight. But there was nothing funny about this new development. The situation had been bad enough when it was just Meredith, but now...an army of demons. This was truly becoming a nightmare.

"Did they hear what her actual plans were? Did she say anything about my dad?" I asked.

Renard spoke up. "No, she didn't go into details about her plans, just that she was creating this army. And no, she didn't mention your dad, but we did see him, and he seemed perfectly fine and happy. Sorry, Rose."

I was grateful for his apology because I had to admit, it would have been a lot easier for me to swallow that Dad had been forced somehow to go with her, but instead it sounded like he was happy to be there. That sucked.

Evie continued, "We also had an incident here tonight. A vampire visiting from Florida bit a demon while in the club. We didn't catch the demon, but we have the vampire chained in the cell below. Once he starts to drift back, we should be able to learn the identity of the demon."

This time everyone's reaction was more depressed than angry, as I think they all assumed Meredith had planted this demon here on purpose. It didn't take much for everyone to realize that things around here were about to change.

I'd recently overheard Evie talking to Christian about having the clan only feed from blood bags until they caught up with Meredith, and now with this new development, I was sure she'd be implementing this new rule. The clan wasn't going to be happy.

"Tomorrow, I will be sending Bobby and Dom back to the hospital to gather more blood bags. We are going to have to restrict ourselves to drinking from them until we can put a stop to these demons. I will not risk one of you becoming infected and falling prey to their mind bond," Evie stated.

See...told you.

"Have you heard back from Balam yet?" Loni asked.

"No. I'm expecting his call tonight. Sunrise is still hours away, so once I receive his call, I'll gather you all again." Evie dismissed everyone and then she and Dax headed into her office, while everyone else moved to the bar to talk with Renard and Loni.

Just as I started to make my way to join them, Christian grabbed my hand and motioned me in the other direction with a nod of his head.

"I need to get out of here. How about we go back downstairs and continue what we started?"

I knew that if I said no now, he'd be confused, but I was already starting to feel guilty for allowing myself to give in earlier. As much as I wanted to fall back into bed with Christian and let him make love to me until the sun started to rise, I just couldn't. It wasn't fair to him.

"I'm sorry, Christian, but hearing about my dad has kind of ruined the mood. Plus, I want to ask Renard some more questions about what else they found out."

He gave me a small smile and nodded his head in understanding. "Alright. Well, I still need to get out of here so I'm going to head back down.

Come find me when you get your answers." He kissed me and then started down the stairs, disappearing under the stage.

I walked towards the clan and scooted onto the red leather bar stool next to Renard. "I'm sorry to bug you, but you said that you saw my dad, right? Did he really seem okay?"

"Yes, we saw him and Meredith sharing...some pizza in their townhome. He seemed perfectly fine and then the next day he woke up and started getting ready for work. Nothing seemed unusual or off with him at all," Renard explained.

"Good. Thank you. That's good to hear." I wasn't sure what other information I expected, but I wished there was more they could've told me. Like maybe whether or not he seemed sad, or if they thought he was thinking about me at all. I knew they were silly questions that had no answers, but I still felt like asking them. Then one pertinent question did strike me. "Do you think he's aware of what Meredith's doing?"

"No, I don't think so. She went to this meeting alone and had a different guy there that was helping her."

Now this was information I could work with. If I could get a hold of my dad and convince him Meredith was up to something shady, maybe he'd leave her without ever getting involved in this whole demon mess. Maybe I could convince him that she was cheating on him with whoever this other guy was.

Now I had a plan.

CHAPTER TWENTY-THREE

The Voices

(Christian)

I couldn't stand to be upstairs a minute longer. Not with all the voices in my head. As I sat there listening to Evie explain what Renard and Loni had found, I started to hear everyone's inner thoughts. I wasn't scanning them, but I think my clairaudient ability was on overload.

I could hear their panic at Evie's announcement. Dom was questioning whether she should take Tori and just run away. Bobby was giving himself a pep talk about how we could "take these demon fuckers out." And Renard and Loni were reliving everything they'd discovered and their conversation regarding what they thought they should do once shit hit the fan.

I didn't want to be hearing any of these things, because for one, it was confusing and was making my head hurt. And two, because it pissed me off to think that anyone in my clan would even think about ditching Evie and the rest of us.

I knew they were all scared because this was something that none of us had ever faced before, but damn it...you don't just run off and leave your clan behind.

As I reached my room, I decided I'd try to gain some control over my new abilities. But the instant I entered my room, I caught the scent of Rose's lingering passion from before and my mind once again shifted to her.

I wished I could've convinced her to come back downstairs with me. But I understood that she needed to talk to Renard about her dad. I knew she still wanted to reach out to him and was desperate to find a way to get him away from

Meredith, but I was getting desperate for us to have some time to ourselves. Desperate to be happy again, like we were before.

I walked over to my desk and pulled out a piece of old tattered stationery and decided to put my thoughts to words.

I'd never been shy about expressing my feelings to Rose, but I needed another outlet to show her how much I still loved her, even if things were chaotic at the moment.

As I concentrated on Rose and thought of the words I wanted to write, I started hearing a whisper in my mind. It sounded like a female voice calling Rose's name. "Rose. Rose?" I looked around and found nothing out of place. So, after pouring my heart out on paper, I finished my letter and put it back in my desk for safe keeping. Then I made my way over to the bed and laid down. It was time to do some meditating and get a grip on these voices...whoever they were.

* * * * *

(Loraine)

Once again I felt myself being pulled back into my ghostly form. But when I opened my eyes and found myself in Rose and Christian's room, and Rose nowhere in sight, I started to panic. "Rose. Rose?" I called out, knowing she couldn't hear me, but I didn't understand how I could be here if she wasn't.

I quickly noticed that Christian, who was sitting at his desk, turned around and examined the room, looking straight in my direction.

Suddenly, I was filled with the knowledge that he was now a Sire and was gifted with extraordinary psychic powers. I floated over to him and looked down at what he was writing and found that it was a love letter to Rose. It must have been his thoughts of her, combined with his psychic abilities that pulled me into form. How interesting.

I continued to watch as he finished his letter and returned it to a box within his desk. Then he laid down on his bed and began to drift into what I recognized as a meditative state. Since I had no control over when I appeared and disappeared, I was stuck watching as he began his deep breathing and relaxation techniques.

Within moments, I felt a chill brush across me. Since I was a ghost, I wasn't sure how that was even possible. Suddenly, Christian opened his eyes and looked directly at me. "Loraine?"

I think if I still had the ability to faint, there would have been a shiny ghost currently laid out on the floor. "Christian. You can see me?"

"Yes. And apparently hear you, too."

I was so excited that I could finally communicate with someone that I flew up to the ceiling and spun around. I hoped this meant that soon I'd be able to talk to Rose and Jeremy again. What a blessing this was.

"Not that I'm not happy to have someone to talk to, but how are you able to see me and hear me when no one else can?"

"I'm sure it has to do with my heightened abilities now that I'm..."

His sentence trailed off and I realized he didn't know the amount of information I'd obtained since being dead. He probably wasn't even sure if I knew what he truly was.

"It's okay. I know everything. You're a vampire and the new Sire, your clan is preparing to face that demon bitch who killed me, and you love my daughter more than you've ever loved anything in all of your six-hundred-plus years." Suddenly I was the one leaving out information. I was well aware that the vampires didn't know about Rose and Jeremy's demon side, and I also knew it wasn't time for that information to be shared.

"Yes. That's right. Now how exactly is it that you're here on this plane?"

"It only started happening recently. I was first pulled into this very room while Rose was crying on the bed. I believe her grief, combined with her thinking specifically about me, pulled my energy to her. I was able to use *my* psychic gift to calm her. I've visited Jeremy too, and had the same effect on him. There seems to be a pattern; they have to be either very angry or thinking specifically about me, then I appear and my ability soothes them."

"Rose never mentioned you had a psychic ability. Did she know about it?"

"No. Neither did Jeremy. But it wasn't something I had to activate or try to use on people; it was just something that happened whenever I walked into a room. People who were upset would calm, and anyone feeling fear would relax when around me."

"Damn. That's a handy ability to have. I wish I'd developed *that* during my triggering."

By now Christian had pushed off the bed and was walking in my direction. I didn't feel the need to move as I knew he'd just pass right through me. Surprise again. He bumped into my arm as he made to step around me.

"Whoa. That's never happened before. Every time I try to touch Jeremy or Rose, my hand just mists through them."

"This whole situation just keeps getting stranger and stranger. I know I'm the new Sire, but honestly, I don't have a clue what to do about any of this. And all I really care about is getting things back to normal with Rose. You probably know this already, but we've been fighting, and there's been some real tension building between us. I just wish there was something I could do to make her happy, if only for a small moment within all this craziness."

As I floated over to the vampire who loved my daughter, I thought of the perfect thing to help get these two back on track. Because regardless of Rose's plans, I somehow *knew* it was vital that she and Christian remain together. I assumed this was more cosmic information the gods felt I needed to know. So, I laid a hand on Christian's shoulder,

still amazed that I could do so, and told him just

what he needed to do.

CHAPTER TWENTY-FOUR

Perfectly Perfect

(Rose)

Though talking to Renard hadn't taken long, I still wasn't ready to head downstairs to find Christian. I'd already made up my mind not to be selfish and allow any more intimacy between us, so I'd wandered around for the next few hours talking and dancing and wasting time with Dominique, Tori, and Loni.

Currently we were upstairs in one of the private rooms talking about how Loni had been turned into a vampire.

"I met Renard when he was visiting Hollywood. I was working at Grauman's Chinese Theatre and he came in doing the tourist thing. He was this cool European guy with spiky hair. He was so hot I wanted to jump him that first night.

From then on, we spent every night together for two weeks straight. Of course at the time, I had no idea he was a vampire. He told me he had to spend his days with his family but that his nights were mine." Loni giggled and continued to reminisce.

"After spending those two weeks with him, I found out that he wasn't just a pretty face, but that he was also really smart and shared my love of architecture. By the end of his vacation, I'd completely fallen in love with him and him with me. He petitioned Evie to change me and she agreed. He told me what he was and that if I accepted to join his clan, we could be together forever. And so I did. That was about eighty-six years ago."

It amazed me that it was that long ago, yet she gushed about him like they'd just met. But, I suppose for a vampire, eighty-six years really was just a drop in the bucket when it came to forever. I almost asked why they waited so long to formally wed, but I didn't want to be rude. Plus I was suddenly depressed because this perfect dream of spending an eternity with the man you loved had almost been mine as well.

I excused myself and headed back downstairs. As I reached the main floor, Evie came out of her office and looked around the club. "Rose, can you please go downstairs and ask Christian to join me in my office?"

"Sure, Evie."

I ran down the spiral staircase and descended into the pit, wondering what Evie wanted to talk to Christian about now. Hopefully she'd heard from Balam and would soon be sharing the news with us all.

When I reached the door to our bedroom I listened for a moment before turning the knob and walking inside. The lights were off and I couldn't see a thing. It was dead quiet. But suddenly there was a click, and the entire room was lit up with sparkling moon and star crystals hanging from the black ceiling.

I fell to my knees and started to cry as I stared up into a replica of my old room.

"I hope you like it. I wanted to do something special to show you how much I love you."

"Oh, Christian." I couldn't even speak as I was wracked with emotion. The sight of this had me missing my mom and falling in love with Christian all over again. I looked up at him sitting on the bed, saw him looking at something off to the side of me and then I flew into his arms. "I love it. I can't tell you how much I love it."

"I'm so glad. When I got the idea a few hours ago, I snuck upstairs through Evie's office and out of the club to go grab everything. They aren't the original ones from your house, but it's all I could do in a rush."

"It's perfect. Perfectly perfect." I couldn't stop crying as I buried my head in his chest. He kissed my hair and continued to hold me. I thought I heard him whisper thank you to someone but wasn't sure as I couldn't hear much over the sound of my sobs.

Once I was able to get myself under control, I looked at all his hard work. He must have used his vampire speed to paint the ceiling because there were little splashes of black paint on the walls where it had splattered from the rushed brush strokes. The crystals were just like the old ones in my room, and they were sparkling in the artificial moonlight that Christian had rigged to shine on them from a new lamp in the corner.

"Christian, I'm sorry for being so distant and angry lately. It's just with everything that's been happening, I've been really sad and emotional. Even though I love you with all my heart, I still miss my mom and dad and my friends. And then when you told me about my dad moving and the other stuff, I just felt angry and betrayed. I know it wasn't your intention to keep things from me, but it's how I felt at the time. Can we just start over, please? I hate fighting with you and I don't ever want to be without you."

Talk about a one-eighty. I knew it was a big risk to change my plans of leaving, but honestly, I didn't care. No matter what happened, I couldn't leave Christian. He was truly the love of my life and whatever we faced, we'd face it together. Now and forever...however long forever ended up being for me. It was worth it. *He* was worth it.

His passionate kiss was all the answer I needed. I started to fall into his arms when I remembered the reason I'd come to find him in the first place. I jumped up from the bed, wiped my face, and pulled myself together. "Wait. Evie sent me to get you. She wants you to come up to her office."

He stood up, grabbed my hand, and kissed me once more. "Alright. Let's go see what Evie has to say. I think we're about to find out exactly how to put an end to Meredith and her fledgling army."

CHAPTER TWENTY-FIVE

Reactions

(Meredith)

All the demons arrived for the meeting right on time. After welcoming everyone, we'd had a great time talking about our heritage and all the stories that had been passed down through the generations of our different families. I tried to hide my impatience and I thought I did a pretty good job, but Damien on the other hand was having a hard time keeping his excitement under control. Twice I had to ask him to join me again as he kept wandering over to the tables.

Finally, I announced, "Everyone, thank you for coming. Now please help yourselves to the wonderful spread we have for your enjoyment tonight."

Damien nodded to each of his relatives that were aware of what they were here for and they each grabbed a glass and filled it with the punch. After slamming back the drink, they all headed towards the alcove as planned.

Damien waited for a few minutes before following them. I stayed to mingle with the others who were unaware of what was happening. They continued to chat, make their plates, and pour their drinks. Once everyone had started to sip from their glasses, I slipped out to check on Damien and the others. "How's it going in here?"

"Good. They've each reported they can feel the effects of the blood, but that it's very subtle. Like they've just chugged an entire energy drink," Damien explained.

"Perfect. We don't want an overwhelming reaction from anyone, so that's really good news.

I'm going back out to monitor everyone else. Let me know if anyone starts to show signs of aggression."

"Sure thing, boss."

As I re-entered the main hall, I watched everyone mill around, working off their nervous energy. The boost they were experiencing from the blood seemed to be the perfect dose. Everyone was happy and seemed to be enjoying how they felt, whether they understood the reason behind it or not. No one was acting strangely or showing any signs of ill side effects...yet. Most of them were still on their first cup of punch. I wondered if we would need to worry once they started having seconds and thirds. Only time would tell.

I watched as Damien and his pack of relatives headed back to the table for refills. I motioned for them to take some food too, so they wouldn't look suspicious. After filling their plates and glasses, they once again headed back to the alcove. I joined them after a few minutes of mingling.

"Any changes?" I asked.

"Yes and no. They still feel like it's just a nice boost of energy that they're getting, but we've tested the effects and watch this."

He motioned to one of his cousins, who picked up a metal folding chair and proceeded to fold the leg in half. It seemed the blood was having a greater effect after all.

"Great. But that needs to be it for tonight. No more tests, and no more refills. Understand?"

"No problem, boss."

The rest of the men nodded their agreement as I headed back out of the room. But as I rounded the corner and took a final glance back at Damien, the angry look on his face had me nervous. These reactions of his were something I was going to have to address soon. Very soon.

(Jeremy)

After my shower, I felt so relaxed that I decided to not even broach the subject of going back to the club with Meredith once she got home. She said she wouldn't be late, but it was already eleven o'clock and I hadn't heard from her. Usually her meetings only lasted an hour and she was home by 10 p.m., so I decided to grab a beer from the fridge and watch TV in bed while I waited up for her.

I still planned on heading to The Rising Pit at some point in the near future, but instead of involving Meredith, I'd just do it on my own. Rose was my daughter and there wasn't anything or anyone who was going to stand in my way when it came to finding her.

Just as I sank into bed and flipped on the TV, my cell phone started vibrating from my nightstand. I picked it up and answered. It was Meredith.

"Hi, honey. It's me. Sorry I'm running late. We had a larger crowd than usual tonight and the clean-up is taking me longer than expected."

"No problem, babe. I'm just drinking a beer and waiting for you to bring your sexy ass home and join me in bed."

"Mmmm. That's all I needed to hear. I'll be out of here in five."

I chuckled as I tossed the phone back onto the table. Once I found my daughter, my life would be perfect once again.

I eased down against my feather pillow and let the sense of calm I was experiencing settle over me. I wasn't much of a drinker, but apparently a beer after a hot shower was just the remedy I needed to ease my stress.

* * * * *

(Loraine)

Once Christian thanked me for my help, I watched as he enveloped my crying daughter in his arms, then I felt myself starting to disappear. But this time it was different.

I didn't completely disintegrate, but instead I felt like I was traveling at light speed—like you used to see on those Star-Trek movies—and in the next second I was hovering over Jeremy as he laid in his bed with a beer in hand.

I hated to admit it but he looked content. I knew I'd never truly have my family back, and all I wanted was for them to be happy. But the thought of Jeremy being happy with the woman who killed me was too much for me to bear. I wished I could figure out how to appear and disappear whenever I wanted, because staring down at my husband knowing he was lying there waiting for my killer to join him in bed had me begging the gods to get me the fuck out of here.

CHAPTER TWENTY-SIX

Confession

(Rose)

As we made our way to Evie's office, I asked Christian if he wanted me to wait outside so they could talk in private. His answer had been no.

So here we sat on the couch in Evie's office as we waited for Dax to join us.

"I assume Christian has shared the good news with you," Evie said with a smile on her face.

"Yes, he did. I'm so happy for him, but I understand that we need to wait to change me and that you don't want me to tell anyone else."

"Thank you for understanding. I just can't risk any of the clan accidentally biting one of Meredith's demons and having that knowledge to share."

Dax entered the office from behind Evie's bookshelf and took a seat in the chair next to the couch. "Terrance and the prisoner have been fed. I couldn't get any more information from Kennedy. His thoughts still remain fuzzy, but Terrance requested that we keep him posted on what we find out from Balam."

"I'm still debating on what we should do with Terrance. I do have a theory and a plan in mind, but I need a little more time before deciding for sure," Evie stated.

She then stood from behind her desk and walked around to join us, taking a seat in the remaining chair. "I did hear from Balam tonight, and what he explained was quite overwhelming. I'm not sure I've even had enough time to wrap my head around it, but here goes."

Evie relayed that after Balam and the elders completed their research, their theory was that since vampires came from Camazotz and demons came from Yum Camil, only a hybrid—a demon/vampire—would be able to kill an immortal demon, which Meredith and her army were quickly becoming.

Apparently, a stronger demon could kill another demon, but since Meredith was currently the strongest demon in existence, and the original Mayan demons were wiped out eons ago, the elders concluded that combining the two races was the only chance we'd have at killing an immortal demon.

Conversation erupted as the three of them tried to riddle out exactly how a vampire was supposed to bite and turn a demon. This theory sounded like an extreme long shot.

"Obviously our first problem is, we have no way of locating a demon. And how in the hell am I suppose to bite a demon and drain him to the point of death without becoming overtaken by the poison in his blood? Then, what happens if I *am* successful at turning him, and he rises with the ability to forge a mind bond with me, therefore gaining control of a Sire. This whole thing sounds completely fucked to me." Christian was frantically pacing and running a hand through his now jet black hair.

It was definitely going to take some serious brainstorming to figure out *exactly* how to make something like this work, but in the end I was confident we'd be successful. But first I had some research to do, and then it appeared I had a major confession to make.

(Meredith)

After almost two hours of mingling and chatting with everyone here, I was extremely pleased with how tonight had gone. No one had showed any signs of aggression from drinking the blood-spiked punch, but everyone seemed to unknowingly enjoy its effects.

I'd begun to clean up and was almost finished when I looked at my watch and noticed it was already getting close to eleven o'clock at night. I picked up my cell and dialed Jeremy to let him know I was running late.

"Hello."

"Hi, honey. It's me. Sorry I'm running late. We had a larger crowd than usual tonight and the clean-up is taking me longer than expected."

"No problem, babe. I'm just drinking a beer and waiting for you to bring your sexy ass home and join me in bed."

"Mmmm. That's all I needed to hear. I'll be out of here in five."

God, I really did love that man. Hearing his voice and imagining him lying naked in bed waiting for me had my thoughts drifting back to earlier tonight. I looked down at my stomach and rubbed a protective hand across it. *I wonder if I'm really pregnant.* It would be my dream come true, but at the same time, I wasn't sure that now was the best timing.

The vampires hadn't come looking for me yet, but I knew it would only be a matter of time before they did. And even though I wasn't planning on being the one to initiate any fighting, I wasn't going to stop forming my army. What was that old saying...the best defense is a good offense?

Well, that was the plan I was actively implementing: create my army and prepare to defend myself and my kind.

As I finished my cleanup, I noticed one last thing I needed to take care of. The chair with the bent leg had found its way out of the alcove and was stacked with the others. I shook my head and grabbed the chair, wondering if all of this was such a good idea after all.

I knew as long as I kept drinking my fill of human blood on a regular basis, I didn't have to worry about any of these boys surpassing me in strength and posing a threat, but I did have to worry about their egos and stupidity. I was going to have to meet with Damien again very soon to make sure he'd be able to keep his cousins in line. Because if he couldn't...I would.

CHAPTER TWENTY-SEVEN

Rules

(Damien)

After the meeting was over, I told Meredith that with her permission I'd like to leave with my cousins in order to keep an eye on them, instead of staying to help her clean up as usual. She thought it was a good idea, waved goodbye, and said she'd give me a call tomorrow.

I was pleased with how the guys were handling the effects of the blood in their systems. But, after Meredith had put down her foot about no more tests earlier, we hadn't been able to find out if everyone in the group had increased in strength, or if it was just Raúl. So, I decided, the hell with Meredith's rules, and we were currently heading to the warehouse to conduct some tests on our own.

I disposed of the woman's body after I finished with her earlier, so that wasn't a concern. Besides, I didn't want to introduce them to killing and feeding directly from a person just yet. I couldn't risk any of my cousins becoming frenzied and growing stronger than myself. Instead, we were just here to test the limits of our strength.

"This is fucking amazing. I'd heard the stories that our ancestors used to drink human blood, but honestly, I just thought it was a crock of shit that fed into the tales of Mayan sacrifices and stuff like that. I had no idea it was true and could have this kind of effect on us," Raúl said.

"I was pretty shocked when Meredith first introduced me to it as well. She's the first of our kind to figure it out and begin the process of turning immortal."

"She's pretty fucking hot, cuz. Have you tapped that yet?" Juan never was known for his tact, so his crass statement didn't surprise me.

"No, Juan. I haven't tapped that yet, but trust me...I plan to." Their laughter and catcalls rang through the warehouse as we made our way inside.

Thinking about how much I wanted Meredith had me ready to demonstrate just how strong I'd become. Strong enough to take out her lame-ass boyfriend, Jeremy, that was for sure. The dip-shit demon who didn't even know what he was. What a joke.

* * * * *

(Terrance)

Watching my new cell-mate drain his blood

bag had me jonesing to get the hell out of here. I

did not play well with others. Especially a strange

vampire who'd drifted dark and was already

demonstrating signs of aggression.

He was pleasant enough when Dax first

brought him into the cell and secured his chains.

But it didn't take long before he started bucking,

growling, and baring his teeth at me. It was like

watching a rabid dog throw a hissy fit.

Since I was able to focus on Meredith and

everything she'd made me do, I knew that all of

her blood had left my body. I wasn't sure why Evie

was still holding me here. I wanted to ask the

question, but already felt bad enough over

everything I'd put them through and didn't want to

be an ass by pressing the matter. I knew she'd let me out sooner or later. I just hoped it was sooner.

I leaned my head back against the cinderblock wall as I closed my eyes, and did the only thing that brought me peace. I started to think about Loraine.

The memories of her were the only thing that had seen me through this entire situation. Once my thoughts had started to clear, I focused on her beautiful face and how her laugh used to make me feel. It was truly a miracle that despite Meredith's manipulations, I'd genuinely fallen in love with her.

She never knew how I felt. She loved her husband, and therefore I chose to keep my feelings to myself. It was so easy and relaxing when we were together, and even though I knew she'd never reciprocate my feelings, it didn't diminish what I felt. There were times I wouldn't even feed from her, but we would just sit and talk instead. I knew if anyone heard me expressing these tender emotions, they would think I was being manipulated again, but that wasn't it. It was just Loraine and how she'd made me feel.

As I sat thinking about our time together, I felt a cool breeze brush past me as I relaxed into my memories. It almost felt as if she was here with me. I laughed at the stupidity of my thoughts. But in my own defense, sitting in a cell, chained to a wall, while listening to an infected vampire rant and rave, was definitely a situation that lent itself to fantasizing about the woman I loved.

* * * * *

(Loraine)

After my plea to the gods, I felt myself start to disintegrate again. Thankfully I was sent whisking through space and escaped Jeremy's bedroom before Meredith came home.

When I felt my ghostly form solidify once again, I opened my eyes and received a surprise. I was in the basement cell of The Rising Pit with Terrance.

I quickly looked around for Rose or Christian, but only saw Terrance and...Kennedy. Yes, there was the information I needed. His name was Kennedy, and he was a vampire who was infected with demon blood. Rose's blood. *Oh crap.*

That still didn't explain why I was here, and then I received another info dump and settled down next to Terrance. The vampire who loved me.

CHAPTER TWENTY-EIGHT

Rose

(Jeremy)

After waiting up for Meredith and welcoming her into our bed as planned, we spent the night in each other's arms and the thought of going back to The Rising Pit never crossed my mind again...until this morning.

I decided it was something I was going to do on my own. I wasn't sure why Meredith was against going to the club, but I didn't want to pressure her to go with me if she didn't want to. And if I was being honest with myself, I didn't really want to hear why she thought it was a bad idea.

I kissed her goodbye as I threw my suitcase into the backseat of my car. I was once again headed to Seela for another business meeting that would keep me overnight. How convenient. The timing of this meeting had me penciling *"Friday night at The Rising Pit"* into my day-planner.

As I made the normal pit-stops on my way out of town—the cleaners, the Coffee Hut, and the Donut Mill—I thought about what I'd say to Rose if I was lucky enough to actually find her.

Obviously, we'd have talk about the accident and why she'd practically gone off the deep end and attacked Meredith. But we'd also have to discuss what was going to happen next.

Since I'd sold the old house and moved in with Meredith, I honestly didn't see my twenty-one year old daughter wanting to live with me and the woman she'd attacked. I could continue to dream about Rose coming back to me, but I had to be realistic, it was something that just wasn't going to happen. But as long as I knew she was okay and that we'd be staying in contact, I supposed it was finally time I let my little girl go.

Halfway into my trip, my cell phone rang, showing a number I didn't recognize.

"Hello. This is Jeremy."

The line was silent. I looked down at the display to make sure I hadn't dropped the call, but it still showed as active. "Hello?" I didn't hear any breathing or background noise at all.

"Hello? Is anyone there?" Again, silence. But, just as I was about to flip the cell closed I heard, "Dad. It's me...Rose."

It was now my turn to be silent. Tears filled my eyes and I eased my car onto the shoulder. "Rose? Honey, is that really you?"

"Yeah, Dad. It's me. Are you alone?"

"Oh, baby, it's so good to hear your voice. And yes, I'm alone. I'm in my car. Where are you? I'm actually headed back to Seela today."

"That's great. I'm still in Seela. Is there any way you could meet me somewhere today?"

"Just tell me when and where."

* * * * *

(Rose)

After listening to Christian, Evie, and Dax argue about the finer points of creating a vampire-demon hybrid for the past two hours, I finally decided to call it a night. Once Christian joined me, he delivered the disappointing news that they were no closer to figuring anything out than they were before.

Well, I had many things of my own to figure out, and my first bit of research was going to involve my dad. I'd warned Christian that I was going to be reaching out to him soon. I just hadn't clarified that I would be doing it tomorrow. I'd decided I would call my dad in the morning and

see if I could arrange a meeting with him during

the day, while Christian and the clan slept. I didn't

think I had anything to worry about from

Meredith because I'd planned to make sure that

Dad would be coming alone.

I snuggled up next to Christian just before he

went comatose. I figured I'd better get a few hours

of sleep before putting my plan in motion. Just the

thought of seeing my dad was exhausting.

Exciting, but exhausting. I knew he'd have tons of

questions, and to be perfectly honest, I didn't

know how I was going to answer any of them. But

I knew it was time, especially with how things were

about to change.

(Christian)

I couldn't believe I'd just become the new

Sire, only to be faced with such an impossible

situation. What Balam and the elders had come up

with as *"our best chance,"* was absolutely ludicrous. I

was pissed at the prospect of having to bite a

demon and risk permanently drifting dark, but the

real problem came from that damn mind bond

they were able to forge. How could we risk a Sire,

any Sire, ending up under the control of a demon?

This simply wasn't going to work. We'd have to

find another way.

I knew my hair and eyes were most likely still

drifting even as I reached my room, but seeing

Rose lying in there with her long blonde hair

splayed over my pillow had me relaxing instantly. I

should have followed her out of Evie's office and

spent that time finishing what we'd started earlier, but I couldn't. I had to stay behind and continue to talk circles about what we should do.

As I laid down next to Rose, I informed her that we hadn't gotten any closer to finding a solution to the problem, then I opened my arms to her, letting her snuggle close.

I wasn't going to let this new problem take the enjoyment out of the simple things like this. Holding the woman I loved as I fell comatose. No matter how bad things seemed, all I had to do was put my arms around her and everything was right in my world once more.

CHAPTER TWENTY-NINE

Puzzle

(Evie)

"I think we have something else to consider here. We know that once the demon blood works its way out of your system, you'll drift back to normal, just like Terrance. And until then, we can just keep you locked up so you won't be a risk."

I was trying to explain to Christian that the risk might be minimal if we planned ahead. If our only hope of destroying a demon was to create a hybrid, then that was exactly what we needed to do. Was it going to be tricky? Yes. But what other choice did we have? Balam had explained that since the old demon gods were no longer present in our world, this was our best chance.

"I understand that you're nervous, and of course, it's not going to be easy. But at least now we have a group of demons to choose from. We'll just follow Renard back to where Meredith conducted her meeting, and then abscond with one of her little members. By the time she misses anyone, it will be too late."

"Evie, it's not that simple. Whether it's my clairsentient ability or something else, I just *know* that it won't work. There's something we're missing, and until I get a clear picture of what that something is...I'm not going to be biting anyone." Christian's statement held the slightest hint of his Sire's command.

As frustrating as all of this was, I was extremely proud of how well he was adjusting, and how powerful a new Sire he was quickly becoming.

"You're right, Christian. We can't rush into anything. The sun is almost up, so let's plan to continue this conversation tomorrow. When you wake, I'd like you to meet me at the cell. We need to see if you can gather any more information from Kennedy, and find out if he's started to drift back yet."

"You think the demon blood has already left his system?" Dax asked.

"Yes, I do. Terrance was feeding from Meredith repeatedly for months, but Kennedy had only a small taste, so if the timing proves accurate, he should be drifting back by tomorrow night."

"Alright, Evie. I'll meet you there. Goodnight."

I watched Christian exit my office and then turned to face Dax. He was still sitting in the chair, gnawing on a plastic toothpick as his hair drifted from dark blonde to the deepest brown. "I don't like this, Evie. None of it seems right. How can creating a hybrid demon really help us? Seems to me, we'd be playing into our own demise."

"I've considered that too, but I have to trust Balam. If he and the elders think this is our best shot, I really don't see any other option. Meredith may not have started anything yet, but it sure as hell seems like she's getting ready to. I won't let her and her army start infecting the vampires in the area. I'll do whatever it takes to protect our clan and our race."

Dax removed the toothpick from his mouth and slowly stood up from the chair. "I know you want to protect us all, but Evie, it's really not up to you anymore. It's Christian's job now, and like he said, he's not going to bite anyone until *he* figures things out. All we can do now is just support him, okay?"

I leaned into his embrace and rested my head on his shoulder. He was right of course. I still held the status of Sire within my clan, but Christian was the true leader now. I just hoped that with all of his abilities, he was able to figure out what piece of the puzzle we were missing, and soon.

* * * * *

(Rose)

I woke up just after 9 a.m., slid out from under Christian's arm, and proceeded to get dressed. I didn't have to worry about waking anyone up, as they were all comatose and would remain so until the sun went down.

As I showered and did my makeup, the butterflies in my stomach started doing flip-flops. I knew I'd need to make the call soon, or I'd risk missing Dad. If he still worked his same schedule, he was usually in the office by 10 a.m.

Even though I knew there was no risk of being interrupted, I decided to head upstairs into the club so I could truly be alone. I was nervous but excited to finally be reaching out to my dad. I glanced at the red numbers of the digital clock hanging above the bar...9:36 a.m. I flipped open my cell and dialed.

"Hello. This is Jeremy."

Tears immediately started streaming down my cheeks at the sound of his voice. I couldn't say anything due to the huge lump presently taking up residence in the middle of my throat.

"Hello?" he repeated. "Hello? Is anyone there?"

I finally got my emotions under control, swallowed, and said, "Dad. It's me...Rose."

The line was silent for a moment as I heard what sounded like a car slowing down then he said, "Rose? Honey, is that really you?"

"Yeah, Dad. It's me. Are you alone?"

"Oh, baby, it's so good to hear your voice. And yes, I'm alone. I'm in my car. Where are you? I'm actually headed back to Seela today."

"That's great. I'm still in Seela. Is there any way you could meet me somewhere today?"

"Just tell me when and where."

"How about the park around the corner from that steak house on Elm and 3rd?"

It was the park where Christian and I had watched a screening of Dracula on the night of our first date. I hadn't thought about that night in so long but it still made me giggle.

"That sounds great. I need to make a couple calls to cancel some meetings today, but I can be there in an hour."

"Wait. You can't call anyone! Dad, no one can know about this...especially Meredith."

The line went dead once again, and I was worried I'd made a mistake by bringing her up. But

I couldn't risk any of her little peons knowing where I was. "Dad, I'm serious. If you don't promise not to call anyone and come alone, you can forget it. I won't come unless you keep it a secret."

After a heavy sigh, he said, "Alright. I'll head straight there and not call anyone. But Rose, I hope you're planning to explain all of this odd behavior."

"I am, Dad. But whether you'll believe me or not is a whole different story."

An hour later I wiped my sweaty palms on my jeans for the umpteenth time as I stood nervously behind a large maple tree watching for my dad's car. I'd driven Christian's car and parked it around the corner. I didn't want my Dad or anyone else seeing it and linking me back to The Rising Pit. As far as he knew, Evie still hadn't seen Christian or me since the accident, and that's exactly how I wanted to leave it in case this meeting didn't go as I hoped.

The second I saw his car, I wanted to run. Run away or run into his arms, I wasn't sure. I was so nervous because deep down I didn't think he'd be listening to a single thing I had to say, which could prove to be a problem, since he'd probably want to grab me and head to the nearest insane asylum.

As he approached the bench, I stepped out from behind the tree. He froze in place, tilted his head, and then opened his arms to me. I went running.

"Dad!"

"Rose, my baby girl. Are you alright?"

"Yes. I'm fine." I pulled out of our embrace and took his hand, then led him over to take a seat on the bench.

He sat there quietly for a few moments just staring at me. "Rose, I've been so worried about you." He hugged me again and this time I didn't pull away. He stroked my hair and rocked me back and forth like I was a baby in his arms. I felt precious to him once again.

"Where have you been? I looked for you everywhere but didn't have any luck."

"Dad, I'm not going to tell you that. I love you and I just need you to know that I really am okay."

He leaned back, and the red sparks that flashed through his eyes were enough to send me into a full blown panic attack. *Holy shit!* What if my dad *was* being controlled by Meredith? What if she'd started to feed him human blood to trigger his demon DNA? Shit, this could be really bad. What the hell had I been thinking?

"Rose, as angry as that makes me, I'm trying

to respect the fact that you're a grown woman and don't need my protection. But I just don't understand why you can't tell me where you're staying. What's with all the secrecy?"

The red sparks left his eyes and he seemed to be relaxed once again. As much as I wanted to head for the hills, I knew that now might be my only chance to try to explain everything and maybe get some answers.

"Okay, Dad. I'll explain everything, but you have to promise to keep an open mind. I'm not crazy, and if you push me, I can prove everything I'm saying, but I'd rather you not force me to."

There. I thought that was a pretty good way to start the conversation.

Dad settled into his seat, getting as comfortable as you could on a park bench, and then began to listen to my wild tale of vampires and demons.

CHAPTER THIRTY

Bombshells

(Loraine)

The moment I materialized and found both Rose and Jeremy sitting in a park, my heart started to break. Seeing my family together had tears running down my ghostly cheeks. I would have given anything to be able to communicate with them, but as usual I couldn't. Christian was still the only one who could see and hear me.

As I moved to hover around the back of the bench, I saw Jeremy's eyes flare red at whatever Rose had just said. I let my hand mist through his shoulder and sensed him immediately relax. I knew my calming energy was going to be in high demand here today, because Rose was about to drop some major bombshells. I listened as she relayed the story of the vampires and demons to her dad.

She proceeded to tell him that his new girlfriend was in fact the demon who killed me, and that both he and Rose were demons too. Despite the skeptical looks that continually swept across Jeremy's face, he kept quiet and allowed Rose to finish her explanation. I was so thankful my calming ability still worked even from beyond the grave.

Rose continued to explain what happened the night she attacked Meredith, and how the bitch was now trying to build an army to fight against the vampires.

(Rose)

"I don't know what to say. I'm trying to wrap my head around this, but demons and vampires— it's just so unbelievable."

"Dad, I told you I could prove it if you need me to, but I had hoped that you'd just trust me instead. Meredith is a demon and so are we. She killed mom and wants me dead too so she can have you all to herself. Did you really never have a clue about what you are?"

"What I am? What I am is your father and someone who goes to work every day to provide a good life for his family. I'm just a normal guy!"

"A normal guy? Is that why just minutes ago you had red sparks shooting through your eyes?"

That must have been the perfect thing to say, because in the next second he scooted closer and grabbed both of my hands. "You noticed my eyes flaring red?"

"Yes. When you got mad. It's a typical demon trait."

"Oh my god. I thought I'd been imagining things. I've been noticing lately that I seem to get angry a lot easier and that when I am mad, my eyes flare red and my temperature starts to rise."

He sagged further onto the bench. I was worried that he was close to passing out. I knew this was a lot for him to take in, not only learning that vampires and demons were real, but learning that his daughter who'd been missing for months, was smack in the middle of it. Yeah, I think I was close to passing out too.

"Dad. You have to get away from her. If she hasn't started slipping you blood yet, I'm sure it's only going to be a matter of time. I don't want you to end up under her control and a part of her stupid demon army. The vampires will have no choice but to destroy you if you do."

"I assume the vampires you're talking about are Christian and his 'family.' I'm not stupid, and I know that's where you've been staying. I suppose I should be grateful to the owner for keeping you safe."

"Yes. I'm staying with Christian and his clan. We are in the process of figuring out how to fight the demons. I want you to come back with me, Dad. I know Evie would let you hide with us. You don't even have to go back to Masen. We could just go back to the club right now."

We sat in silence for what seemed like minutes. I didn't have anything else to say and I knew Dad needed some time to let this all sink in. I hated that our first conversation, after being apart for months, was about demons and vampires instead of how much I missed him and how happy I was to see him. But with the situation escalating like it was, it was something that couldn't be avoided.

"Rose. I love you, and I'm trying here, I really am. But I can't just walk away from Meredith without at least confronting her about all this. I want to believe you, but at the same time I don't. I can't stand the thought that I've soiled your mother's memory by falling in love with the woman who killed her. And if what you're saying really is true, then I *need* to face Meredith and put things to an end once and for all.

"No! Dad, you can't. If she finds out you know about her and that you're aware of your heritage, she could hurt you, or even kill you. Especially when you tell her you're leaving. No.

Please just come with me." I frantically grabbed a hold of his arms, but he shook me off.

"I can't, baby girl. Facing her is a risk I have to take. I know you said you can prove everything to me, but I need this...I need to prove it to myself. I'll call you tonight."

I sat with tears running down my face as my dad kissed the top of my head and headed back towards his car. *What have I done?* I thought that by telling him everything, I could convince him to come with me so he'd be safe. But instead, here I sat watching him walk off to meet his death.

CHAPTER THIRTY-ONE

Questions and Confessions

(Christian)

When I woke, even though Rose was the first thing to enter my mind, she was nowhere in sight. I assumed she'd already headed upstairs to spend some of her day out in the sun. I worried about her being outside alone, but I couldn't blame her for wanting to take advantage of it while she could. Becoming a vampire and never having that opportunity again was something she'd soon be facing.

I dressed in a hurry and headed to meet Evie outside of the cell as planned. I assumed she'd want me to see if I could obtain the identity of the demon that Kennedy had bitten, but when I rounded the corner, I knew something major was going on and that I wouldn't be getting any information from our prisoner today...or possibly ever.

Everyone was gathered outside of the cell, including Terrance.

"What's going on? And no offense, man...but why is Terrance out of his chains?" I asked.

"Terrance has drifted back to normal and I no longer fear Meredith's control over him. Plus...look at Kennedy," was Evie's deadpan response.

I glanced into the cell to find Kennedy practically foaming at the mouth and straining against his chains so hard that they were beginning to dig into his skin. He hadn't started to drift back as Evie assumed he would and now I suddenly realized the seriousness of the situation.

"How is it that Terrance has drifted back but Kennedy hasn't?"

"That's the question isn't it? There's something about what happened to Terrance that's different than what's happening to Kennedy. Terrance was never like that, even when he drifted to his darkest point," Evie replied.

She was right. There was something special about Terrance's recovery that we weren't understanding. And we'd better figure it out fast, because if Kennedy didn't start to show signs of improvement soon, we'd be forced to deliver the true death.

"Let's all go upstairs. I have a lot of information to share with you and we need to talk this out as a group," Evie directed.

We all climbed the spiral staircase and emerged from under the stage only to find Rose sitting on the floor by the front door crying her eyes out.

I rushed to her side and wrapped her in my arms. "Baby, what's wrong? Are you hurt?"

"No," she sobbed. "But I did something stupid and I think my dad could die because of it."

Everybody slowly took seats at sporadic tables around the club. It looked like tonight was shaping up to be full of questions and confessions. "What did you do, Rose? What's happening with your dad?"

"I went to meet him today, and I told him about Meredith and the war that's coming between the demons and vampires. I told him she killed Mom and that was the reason I attacked her. I'd hoped that he'd come back here with me to stay safe, but he said that he had to confront Meredith and put an end to things."

She threw herself fully into my arms and I tried to absorb the shakes that were now wracking her entire body. "Oh, Christian. What have I done? I just wanted him to come here with me to be safe, and now she's probably going to kill him when he tries to leave her. I'm so stupid. I should have listened to you. I'm so sorry."

I looked up to find everyone in the club staring at us with concerned looks on their faces. But the face I most wanted to see wasn't there. So I concentrated and called out with my mind. *"Loraine? Rose needs you."*

As soon as I opened my eyes, her ghostly form was hovering over us and she was laying a misty hand on Rose's back. "There, there, baby girl. Everything will be alright," I heard her say.

"Are you sure? Is there any way you can go make sure Jeremy will be safe?" I asked the question in my mind, and thankfully she seemed to hear me because she nodded and disappeared.

Her presence did the trick because Rose sat up and wiped the tears from her face, then spoke to the entire clan. "I'm very sorry for not listening to Christian and Evie's advice. I hope I haven't made things worse by telling my dad of your existence, but I didn't think there was any other way to explain what happened. I understand if you no longer wish me to be part of your clan."

Evie stood and made her way over to us. She took Rose's hands and helped her to her feet. "Rose, we all understand your need to keep your dad safe. But please understand that the safety of my clan comes first, which I already consider you a part of. So while I'm not mad at you, I do expect you to follow our requests. We wouldn't ask these things of you if they weren't important."

I wanted to grab Rose and speed out of the club and into the night. I knew Evie had every right to say those things to her, but I couldn't help feeling like I needed to protect her from the reprimand. "Baby, we'll talk about this later. But

I'm sure you're dad will be okay. Can you trust me when I tell you I *know* things will work out?"

"Yes, Christian. I trust you," Rose answered.

We took seats at the table with Renard and Loni, and waited for Evie to begin her long explanation of what we'd learned from Balam.

The conversation had gone just as I'd expected; everyone started yelling and arguing how we were screwed since we didn't even have a Sire to create a hybrid.

I kept watching Evie, expecting her to let everyone in on our secret but she didn't. When those arguments died down, we finally got to the part of the discussion I was currently most interested in: trying to figure out how Terrance had drifted back when it was becoming apparent that this wasn't normally how things worked.

"I have a theory about how Terrance was able to drift back after being infected," Evie announced. "I briefly spoke to Terrance and Rose about it, and it seems like the only logical explanation to this illogical situation."

Everyone looked back and forth between Terrance and Rose, with confusion on their faces. Even I was wondering how the two of them had anything to do with his ability to drift back.

"While Terrance was under Meredith's control, he somehow fell in love with Rose's mother, Loraine. I think that being in love, and still retaining access to those feelings throughout his infection, is the real reason he's been able to drift back."

Everyone's shocked reactions floated through the air. Once again I'd forgotten that Terrance had admitted to being in love with Loraine. It made perfect sense though. Love was a human emotion: one that kept the light in our souls alive. That light must be the key factor in beating back the demon infection. Love...I guess it really does conquer all.

"I don't think it's enough to have the demon blood clear out of your system alone. I think you have to have that spark of love still touching your soul in order to be brought back to the light," Evie finished.

Terrance smiled at Rose, and she smiled back. I'm sure it was still awkward to know that someone other than her father had been in love with her mom. But it seemed to be a good thing in the end. Loraine's influence really did touch everyone she was around, and I hoped right now she was using her ability to keep Jeremy safe.

CHAPTER THIRTY-TWO

Explain

(Jeremy)

Seeing Rose had been wonderful and terrible at the same time. I was so happy she was safe, but after everything she'd told me, I was left so confused; I just didn't know what to do.

According to her, I'd been sleeping with the woman who killed Loraine, and my little girl and I were both demons. I would have never believed her story except that she knew about the red sparks that flared in my eyes whenever I got angry. I'd known all along that something strange was happening, but admitting I was a demon was a pretty big pill to swallow.

I cancelled my business meetings and headed back towards Masen. I had to confront Meredith about all of this, even if it was going to be the death of me. At this point I truly didn't care whether I lived or died. How could I? I was so disgusted with myself for falling in love with the woman who killed my wife. I knew Rose was going to be fine on her own, so really...what did it matter how any of this turned out for me?

I thought about the best way to approach the subject with Meredith all the way home, but when I reached our house, I didn't have to ponder any longer. There was a blue Ford truck parked in our driveway, so I decided to leave the car on the street and snuck my way into the house through the back door.

I immediately heard noises coming from the garage. When I opened the door just a crack I was hit with a coppery smell that made my stomach roll.

It was blood. I was sure of it.

As quietly as I could, I inched the door open to get a better look.

Suddenly I wished I was at The Rising Pit with my daughter and her vampire friends, because what I saw had me scared to death. Meredith was standing behind a man with her teeth sunk deep into his neck. Blood was gushing from the wound and down the front of his shirt. His eyes were wide with shock as she continued to gulp down his blood.

I was frozen in place, unable to breathe or move. If this was what being a demon meant, I wanted nothing to do with it. And I certainly wanted nothing to do with her.

When I couldn't stand to look any longer, I started to retreat as silently as I could. Apparently I wasn't silent enough, because the door flew open and Meredith stood in front of me, blood dripping down her mouth onto the tiled kitchen floor.

"Jeremy!" She quickly wiped the blood from her mouth using the sleeve of her shirt. "What are you doing home? Oh my god, please Jeremy, let me explain. I can explain everything."

Here I stood, scared to death, but it sounded like Meredith was just as terrified as I was.

"I don't want to hear anything you have to say. I know everything, and I'm leaving."

"No. Please don't go. You have to let me explain." Tears were actually running down her face.

"Explain what? Explain that we're demons and you kept it from me? Explain that you killed my wife in order to be with me? Explain that you purposely ran my daughter off so you could have me all to yourself? What the fuck is there left to explain, Meredith?" I was sure my eyes were pure red, and I didn't care. I let the anger build, for once not worrying about what happened when it did.

"Yes, I've lied to you. I knew from the moment I met you that you were a demon. I was so thrilled to have finally found someone like me that I did the unthinkable. I never expected to fall in love with you, but once I had, I couldn't live without you." She had fallen to her knees and tears continued to stream down her face.

"I love you so much and I'm so sorry for everything I've done, but Jeremy, please. You can't leave me."

"Watch me." I began to storm upstairs to gather my things when she said the one thing that stopped me in my tracks.

"Please, Jeremy. You don't understand. You can't leave me...I'm pregnant."

* * * * *

(Meredith)

Earlier today, after Jeremy left for yet another business trip, I called Damien to invite him over. I wanted to know exactly how the rest of his evening had gone once he'd left the meeting with his cousins. I hadn't heard any suspicious new reports other than that of a missing woman, so I was optimistic they hadn't gone off on a killing spree after all.

It was one o'clock in the afternoon when I finally heard Damien's truck pull up to the house.

I invited him in and we sat down to enjoy the small lunch I'd prepared. "So, how did last night go? Any problems with your cousins?"

"No. No problems at all."

I was a little suspicious of his answer as he wouldn't look me in the eye, but instead kept his head bent towards his plate. "So, no side effects or problems with aggression?"

He picked up his sandwich and took a bite, shaking his head as he mumbled, "Nope."

I wasn't buying it. "Alright. What really happened? You're never this quiet when it comes to the effects of the blood, so spill. What aren't you telling me?"

I knew I'd busted him when his shoulders dropped and he let out a long sigh. *Dammit.* My morning had been going so well, and I didn't want anything to ruin it now. I was going to be pissed if I had to go clean up some horrible mess of dead bodies somewhere.

"We didn't do anything wrong, I swear. We just went to an old warehouse and tested out everyone's strength. Raúl was able to bend the chair at the meeting but none of the others got to demonstrate their new abilities, so we just ran some tests of our own."

Phew. That was a relief. I could handle boys being boys, but if they started leaving a trail of bodies, I'd be putting an end to Damien and his cousins really fast. "Alright. No more tests without me being there. And definitely no feeding on the side. I think last night went really well, and doling out the blood in small amounts seems to be the way to go."

Even though he nodded his head and smiled in agreement, the look in his eyes had me wondering if I already had a problem with my second in command. If he was feeding on the side, that meant he could soon be as strong as me, and that was something I couldn't allow. "When's the last time you had any blood?"

"Last night at the party. Same as the others," he responded.

I squinted and tried to focus on his pulse to see if it was racing, which was a telltale sign of lying. And of course...it was. "Why are you lying to me?"

I flew from the chair and had my hands around his throat a second later. I drug him out into the garage and threw him across it. He slammed into the metal cabinet, putting a dent in it. *Shit.* How would I explain that to Jeremy?

"What the fuck, Meredith? Why does it matter if I have a little sip on the side once in a while? Are you worried I'll become more powerful than you?"

I knew in that moment I'd have to end Damien. Not only was he not following my directions, but it was obvious by his statement that he was planning to overthrow me. "You'll never be as powerful as I am. Especially now that I'm pregnant with Jeremy's child."

It was true. I was officially pregnant. I really had been glowing and feeling more powerful, so I'd taken a test just this morning and confirmed the reason why. I was having Jeremy's baby.

The howl Damien let out as he stood up from the garage floor was loud enough to shake the walls. "No! No fucking way will I let you carry that lame-ass demon's baby. What the fuck do you see in him, Meredith? He doesn't even know who he is. I'll kill him the second I see him and then you and I can be together like we should be. Two powerful demons together, ruling as one."

"*I'll kill him the second I see him*" were the only words ringing in my ears as I flew across the garage and landed behind Damien. I struck so fast that he had no idea what was happening. In the next second, I'd buried my teeth deep into his neck and began to drink him dry. I wouldn't have to worry about a mind bond being forged because he wouldn't be walking away from this.

No one threatens Jeremy and my happiness and lives to tell about it.

CHAPTER THIRTY-THREE

Blood Bond

(Meredith)

As I stood there sucking the blood from Damien's neck, I heard a small noise at the door. I looked up to see Jeremy slowly turning away. *Oh God, no!*

I ran to the door. "Jeremy!" I wiped the blood from my mouth in a desperate attempt to salvage an appearance of normalcy, then pleaded, "What are you doing home? Oh my god, please Jeremy, let me explain. I can explain everything."

He stood frozen in place for only a moment then said the words that unhinged my heart. "I don't want to hear anything you have to say. I know everything, and I'm leaving."

"No. Please don't go. You have to let me explain." The tears had started to pour and I fell to the floor as I listened to him yell at me.

"Explain what? Explain that we're demons and you kept it from me? Explain that you killed my wife in order to be with me? Explain that you purposely ran my daughter off so you could have me all to yourself? What the fuck is there left to explain, Meredith?"

I wanted to crawl to him, hold onto him and never let go. But I didn't want to risk him running away before I could explain, so instead, I remained shuddering on the floor.

"Yes, I've lied to you. I knew from the moment I met you that you were a demon. I was so thrilled to have finally found someone like me that I did the unthinkable. I never expected to fall in love with you, but once I had, I couldn't live without you. I love you so much and I'm so sorry for everything I've done, but Jeremy, please. You can't leave me."

"Watch me." He turned to go upstairs and my panic reached its peak.

"Please, Jeremy. You don't understand. You can't leave me...I'm pregnant." I knew it was a long shot he'd give a damn about a demon baby he didn't ask for and probably wouldn't want, but it was my only shot at stopping him from racing upstairs and then straight out of my life.

So while he remained in place with his back to me, I told him about the baby. Then I told him a lie. "I'm pregnant, Jeremy, and once the baby was conceived, it started to draw on the life force of each of us. It's a blood bond they need to survive. If you leave and the baby doesn't have both his parents to draw from...it could die. Please, Jeremy. I know you'll never love me again, but please don't kill our baby by walking away from me now."

I knew he'd have no clue as to whether or not I was telling the truth, but I hoped the idea of hurting an innocent child would be enough of a reason to make him stay. He was such a wonderful man who would never hurt anyone, so I thought I had a good chance at making this work. But as he stood unmoving, still facing away from me, his next words brought that dream to a screeching halt.

"Meredith. You're a demon, a liar, and a murderer. You killed my wife and framed my daughter. How can you possibly think I would give a damn about you and that baby?"

Dammit! He was leaving me with no choice. As he started to turn around, I grabbed the pan from the kitchen counter. Scaling back my strength so I wouldn't kill him, I smacked Jeremy in the head, knocking him unconscious. I just needed some time to think. I loved him with all my heart, and I wasn't ready to give up on my happily ever after just yet.

It didn't take me long to decide what to do. Honestly, it was the only thing I could do if I wanted to keep him here with me, and never have to worry about him leaving again. I dragged him across the kitchen floor and leaned him against the wall, then grabbed a knife from the drawer and used it to nick my wrist. After lightly patting his cheeks, he started to move just enough to indicate he was coming to. That's when I placed my wrist to his mouth and smiled as he began to swallow my blood.

* * * * *

(Loraine)

I materialized into a room full of vampires and Rose crying in Christian's arms. I ran my hand down her back, trying to comfort her as I was filled with the knowledge of why she was in such pain. "There, there, baby girl. Everything will be alright."

"Are you sure? Is there any way you can go make sure Jeremy will be safe?" I knew Christian was speaking into my mind and was worried that Rose was right. Jeremy could be walking straight to his death. I nodded and in the next moment disappeared.

At first I was excited because I thought I'd figured out how to go wherever I wanted, but instead, it turned out that Jeremy's anger and fear levels were what had called me to his side once more. When my body reformed, I was in Jeremy and Meredith's townhome.

He was peeking through the door that led from the kitchen into the garage. Suddenly I had a mental picture of everything that was happening on the other side of the door. I'd never wanted anything more in my entire life than to be able to help my husband escape this evil woman.

I hovered over Jeremy as Meredith came bursting into the kitchen, and then in a flurry of blood and tears proceeded to tell Jeremy that she loved him, and that she couldn't lose him now because she was pregnant.

I wasn't sure if ghosts could pass out, but I must've disappeared when my anger took complete control of me. That was the only time my calming ability didn't work...when *I* was the one who needed it most.

When I finally rematerialized, I found Jeremy sitting on the edge of his bed with Meredith lying next to him. He was holding his cell phone in his hand, and I knew in that second he was preparing to break the news to Rose.

CHAPTER THIRTY-FOUR

Revelation

(Christian)

After Evie's announcement about love being the necessary ingredient to turn a dark-drifted vampire back to normal, everyone dispersed and went downstairs to feed. Evie still wouldn't risk us accidentally feeding on a demon, so we were stuck with bagged blood for the time being.

As the rest of the gang headed towards the stairs, Evie motioned for me to join her in her office instead. I took Rose's hand and let Evie lead the way.

"I think we're going to have to deliver the true death to Kennedy. With what we know now, if he hasn't drifted back already, I don't think he will."

I knew Evie wanted me to be the one to do it. Even though she still carried the poison of true death, this was her way of letting me take charge of the clan, even if it was just between us.

I didn't want to let her down. "Let's wait until the others are done feeding and we'll go down while they open the club. Rose, you don't have to be there with us. You can wait in our room if you'd like, or stay up here with Dax and the others." I didn't want her bearing witness to any more death than she already had.

"Okay. I'll just stay up here with the others." She squeezed my hand and smiled at me with reassurance in her eyes. She knew I was nervous without me even needing to say so. *God, I love her.*

We sat in Evie's office and continued to talk about all the recent events while we waited for everyone to re-emerge from the pit: Terrance being in love and drifting back; Balam's and the elders' assumption that creating a hybrid was the answer to our demon problem; Meredith's reasons for creating her army; and everything else that had come up lately.

Finally, we heard the stage lock into place, indicating that everyone was once again upstairs and starting to open the club. Rose stood up, kissed me, hugged me tight, and then walked out of the office without saying another word. I think she was just as nervous about this as I was.

"Are you ready?" Evie asked.

"Yes." And I was. I'd finally started to trust and enjoy my new abilities. I knew without a doubt how to deliver the true death, even though I'd never done it before. I also knew without a doubt that we had no choice. Kennedy wasn't going to drift back.

I walked to Evie's bookcase and pushed the button to open the door to her secret entrance into the pit. We remained silent as she followed me down the stairs.

Once we reached the cell, we found Kennedy crouched on the floor finishing off the remainder of his blood bag. I didn't hesitate or try to make conversation. I just flew into the cell and grabbed the vampire by the throat and struck.

As I sank my fangs into Kennedy's neck, I released the poison of true death into his system. I pulled away as the poison began to spread through his veins.

As I backed out of the cell to stand next to Evie, I watched as the dark green poison crept across his skin, paralyzing him while turning his body to stone. When I reached her side she said nothing, but instead took my hand as we continued to stare at the green tendrils that were making their way to his heart.

Once the poison reached and solidified his heart, he simply turned to dust. The chains clattered to the ground and Kennedy was gone.

"He didn't suffer, Christian. Once the poison takes hold, it paralyzes them and they don't feel anything." Evie was trying to pull me away from the cell, but I wasn't ready to go just yet.

"I know, Evie. Thank you. But can you please just give me a moment? I'll be up shortly."

She hugged me and left me alone. Or what I thought was alone.

"So, you're officially the new Sire now?" Terrance came sauntering down the hall from the direction of the supply room. I guess not everyone had finished feeding and returned to the club. *Damn.*

"I suppose the evidence speaks for itself." I pointed to the dust pile that used to be Kennedy. I hoped Evie was right about Terrance, and he no longer retained any connection to Meredith through that fucking mind bond. I really didn't want to have to kill him too.

"That's good. I'm glad. You'll make a great Sire, Christian."

His response caught me off-guard. I thought he'd be an asshole about it, but then I realized this *new* Terrance must be coming from the calming effect Loraine had on him.

My god, that's it! That explains why he was able to fall in love with her despite Meredith's manipulations.

Loraine's ability allowed Terrance to retain that connection to his soul, and therefore fall in love with her. He must've always felt at peace when he was near her, which led to him developing feelings for her. In spite of everything, it was a blessing that Loraine had been the one Terrance had targeted. If it'd been anyone else, we would have lost him for sure.

I smiled and thanked him for his kind remarks, and silently sent a thank you to Loraine as well.

"Evie wants to keep it under wraps though, so we can use it to our advantage against the demons. I need you to not say anything to the rest of the clan."

"No problem, but if you want to use your command to guarantee it, I'm okay with that." Again, his response wasn't something I expected, but it seemed genuine so I decided not to use my Sire abilities to guarantee his silence. Besides, this could be the test that proved whether he was still under Meredith's influence or not.

As he followed me up into Evie's office, I began to wonder why Loraine wasn't here with Terrance now. She said that she always appeared when someone was specifically thinking of her, so I figured that's why she'd been drawn to Terrance so much lately. He was probably always thinking about her.

As I shut the bookcase behind us, I suddenly got the overwhelming feeling that something terrible had just happened. As we emerged from Evie's office into the club, I noticed Rose was standing in the middle of the room while everyone else was busy doing their usual prep work.

She was speaking on her cell phone, and in the next moment Loraine appeared above her with a terrified look on her face. Rose threw her phone across the room and it smashed to pieces against the far wall. Then she let out a scream that was so loud, it had everyone frozen in shock.

I watched in horror as the love of my life started throwing chairs and upending tables in a fit of rage I never thought her capable of. "Rose, my god, what's wrong?"

When she spun in my direction, my heart dropped into my stomach. Her eyes were glowing a fiery red.

Time stood still as Loraine explained to me that yes, Rose and Jeremy were both demons, but that they'd only found out recently, and that's why Rose had been pulling away. She wanted to protect me and my clan by leaving. She continued to fill me in on why Rose's anger had finally been released; Jeremy was choosing to stay with Meredith because she was pregnant with his child. Their demon child.

The next bit of divine knowledge I received was from my own psychic abilities. I knew unequivocally that turning Rose was the only thing I could do. To save her, to save us, to save her dad.

Without a moment's hesitation, I flew across the room and sunk my teeth into her neck.

Everything started to become hazy as I heard Evie scream in the background. "Christian, NO!!!"

CHAPTER THIRTY-FIVE

Decision

(Christian)

I always knew Rose would become my consort, but what I didn't know until the decision was made, was that by turning her...she would also become our hybrid.

As I drank from Rose, bringing her to the brink of death, all my thoughts were fuzzy from the effect her blood was already starting to have on me.

I knew for Rose to become my consort I needed to perform the consort ceremony while delivering the sedative of eternal life. So as I settled into my subconscious, I began to think the words that would seal our consort bond, layering them with my Sire command. *"Your life to me, my life to you, through this bond our love is true. Whatever shall come, we share in whole. Life to death, eternity our goal."*

I felt the scanning ability snap into place for Rose as I fell to the ground with her in my arms.

＊ ＊ ＊ ＊ ＊

(Rose)

After leaving Christian behind in Evie's office, I started to help set up the tables and chairs in the club. Suddenly, I felt my phone vibrating and looked down to see my dad's number.

The relief I felt was so overwhelming that I snapped the phone open, buzzing with excitement. "Dad. You're alright?"

"Yes, Rose. I'm fine."

"Oh, thank god. I was so worried that crazy bitch would hurt you when you told her you were leaving. Are you on your way to The Rising Pit now?"

A knot in my stomach started to form when the line remained silent for just a little too long. "Rose, I need you to listen to me, baby. I know this will be hard to understand, but...I'm staying with Meredith. We're having a baby."

No words could flow past the anger now rising within me. I knew without a doubt Meredith had somehow tricked my dad into staying with her. *That bitch is going to pay.*

I didn't even bother hanging up the phone, but instead threw it across the room and watched it smash into tiny pieces.

I knew this was the end for me as I couldn't control my demon side any longer. I started seeing red as I threw chairs and smashed tables. I didn't care if everyone knew, because the second I left here, I'd be going to kill Meredith and would probably never return anyway.

Suddenly from behind me I heard Christian's voice. "Rose, my god, what's wrong?"

I spun around, trying to catch my breath and stared at him with my glowing red eyes. Even though I was angry, the sight of him had me wishing I had time to explain and apologize for everything. But I didn't.

Everyone was staring at me, and just as I prepared to run for the door, Christian was flying at me with his vampire speed.

The next thing I knew was the feeling of his fangs sinking into my neck as I heard Evie scream, "Christian, NO!!!"

I had no control over my body going limp as the man I loved drank the life from me. Suddenly I heard Christian's voice layering my mind. *"Your life to me, my life to you, through this bond our love is true.*

Whatever shall come, we share in whole. Life to death,

eternity our goal."

As I started to take my last breath, I felt a strange snap in my mind as we fell to the floor. The last thing I heard was Christian's voice inside my head. "Rose, I forgive you."

Look for other books in The Rose Trilogy

at Amazon.com, Barnes & Noble, and other online

vendors

Scent of a White Rose – Book 1
(Available Now)

Roses & Thorns – Book 1.5
(Available Now)

Death of a Black Rose – Book 3
(Available 2013)

by

Tish Thawer

Praise for *Scent of a White Rose*

"...everything about *Scent of a White Rose* was such a fresh new concept when it came to vampires, actually it was just a whole new concept in general for the paranormal genre! This is a read any paranormal lover should read!" ~ YA-Aholic

"Tish adds her own unique spin that makes Rose and Christian's story intriguing. The plot twists will definitely have you turning the pages to see what is going to happen next." ~ The Book Lovers Realm

"*Scent of a White Rose* is not the plain Jane girl meets vampire and falls in love story...I will tell you that you should add this book to your TBR list." ~ The Book Nympho

"Thawer managed what I thought was an impossible feat. She was able to put yet another new spin on the age old vampire tale." ~ The Bookshelf Sophisticate

Praise for *Roses & Thorns*

"I totally fell in love with the characters, the action, the writing style, the plot..." ~ Proserpine Craving Books

"If you're a romantic at heart you'll love this forbidden vampire romance filled with emotion and enchanting characters. Roses & Thorns is the perfect follow up to the first book in the Rose Trilogy..." ~ Romancing the Darkside

"I have lost count of all the things I love about this short story. The imagery she used to describe the tender relationship between Rose and her mother Loraine is breathtaking. It is truly heartwarming and will leave you wanting more." ~ The Booklovers Realm